Seasons of Love

...interesting how a timeline was set up with each of the chapters by month and year...the reader could sympathise with the difficulties they faced that threatened their lives together... ~ *Fallen Angel Reviews*

...absolutely outstanding second instalment of Carol Lynne's *Seasons of Love* serial... The cliffhanger of an ending will leave fans clamouring for the next novel in this engaging series. ~ *BlackRaven's Reviews*

Again, depth of characterisation makes this story stand out...sexual scenes are well tied into the overall conflict between the two heroes... ~ *Whipped Cream Reviews*

It was nice seeing how Ms. Lynne developed Nash and Sidney's relationship...all the components needed for a story that I'll be reading again in the future...
~ *Literary Nymphs Reviews*

Total-E-Bound Publishing books by Carol Lynne:

Campus Cravings Volume One: On the Field
Coach
Side-Lined
Sacking the Quarterback

Campus Cravings Volume Two: Off the Field
Off Season
Forbidden Freshman

Campus Cravings Volume Three: Back on Campus
Broken Pottery
In Bear's Bed

Campus Cravings Volume Four: Dorm Life
Office Advances
A Biker's Vow

Campus Cravings Volume Five: BK House
Hershie's Kiss
Theron's Return

Campus Cravings
Live for Today
Incoming Freshman

Good-Time Boys
Sonny's Salvation
Garron's Gift
Rawley's Redemption
Twin Temptations

Cattle Valley Volume One
All Play & No Work
Cattle Valley Mistletoe

Cattle Valley Volume Two
Sweet Topping
Rough Ride

Cattle Valley Volume Three
Physical Therapy
Out of the Shadow

Cattle Valley Volume Four
Bad Boy Cowboy
The Sound of White

Cattle Valley Volume Five
Gone Surfin'
The Last Bouquet

Cattle Valley Volume Six
Eye of the Beholder
Cattle Valley Days

SUMMER

Dedication

As always, my thanks to Drew Hunt
and Theresa A.

Chapter One

After sliding into home plate, Grady Nash stood and brushed the dirt off of his pants. The whoops of the small crowd made him feel like a million bucks. He tipped his KC Royals baseball hat to the folks in the bleachers as he walked back to the bench. Trading his beloved cowboy hate for a baseball hat had been tough, but after numerous comments from the guys he worked with, Nash had found it easier to just relent.

"Not bad for an old man," Butch Carlisle said with a slap on the back, nearly knocking Nash to the ground.

"I'm thirty-four," Nash reminded his new friend.

"Yeah, like I said, old." Butch spat a sunflower seed shell on to the ground, the pile growing with each inning of the softball game. Despite his rough appearance, Butch was an okay guy. With shoulders as broad as a barn and forearms the size of Popeye's, Butch's shaved head only added to the biker exterior he liked to cultivate.

Nash crossed his arms and leant back against the dugout's chain link fence. Despite Butch's barbs, Nash felt damn good. He might be older than the others on the team, but he was still young enough to keep up with them.

"We're going to Wally's after the game," Butch said as another shell flew from his mouth.

"Wally's, huh?" Nash tried to remember what time Sidney had said he'd be home. "I could use a beer." *Or four.* He'd lived in Lake Forest for almost three months and had yet to go out without Sidney, which meant he rarely went out. He'd been lucky one of the guys from the garage hadn't been able to complete the summer softball season or he'd never have left the house that day.

Joe Banks crossed home plate standing up and Nash gave Butch a high five at the come from behind win. Nash followed the rest of the players out of the dugout to acknowledge the effort of the opposing team with hand slaps.

He returned to the bench and picked up his glove. Unlike the other players on the team, Nash didn't own any equipment besides the old beat-up glove he'd used in high school. "I'll follow you," he told Butch as they headed to the parking lot.

Nash climbed into his red Ford pickup. He'd need to call home as soon as he got to the bar. Was it a bad thing that he secretly hoped Sidney was still at the job site? It wasn't that he didn't love Sidney's company, but he was ready to make a few friends of his own. The guys at the garage, where he'd finally found a job, had been pretty good about welcoming him, but Nash wanted more than that. He'd got used to life on the ranch where camaraderie seemed to come naturally. It wasn't that he was looking for a new best friend —

Sidney would forever hold that position in his life—but he enjoyed watching the men at the garage laugh and tease each other. A part of Nash wanted that kind of relationship with them as well.

One beer, he told himself. Surely he'd still get home long before Sidney.

Nash pulled up his truck beside Butch's old-style Harley. He'd driven by Wally's every day going to work but had never been inside. The moment he stepped foot in the door, he smiled. Yeah, he could be comfortable in the place. Not too crowded but with a nice blend of customers, Wally's seemed like an unpretentious spot to grab a beer with friends.

After a quick phone call home to leave a message on the answering machine, he joined the group of guys from the garage, who were busy shoving tables together. The arrangement seemed not only natural for them but the waitress as well. "How many?" she asked, cruising by the group.

"Four to start," Butch said. He turned to Nash. "You like Coors Light?"

Nash nodded, grabbing a paper menu from the centre of the table. "Anything good to eat?"

"Best cheddar burgers in the state," Pauly said.

A frosty mug was set in front of Nash. "You're new," the waitress said.

Nash smiled. "Just moved to town a few months ago from Kansas."

"My name's Jes if you need anything."

"Nash," he said introducing himself. "And I'll take a cheddar burger medium well when you get the chance."

"Steak fries or onion rings?" she asked as she continued to unload the tray of glasses.

"Fries." He held his mug out to Butch who filled it to the rim with beer. "Thanks."

Nash settled in to listen to the rest of the guys dissect the game. He welcomed his dinner with enthusiasm and moaned each time he took a bite. Sidney would enjoy them, he knew that, but once again Nash felt selfish enough to keep the information to himself.

"You married?" Joe asked Nash.

Nash wiped his mouth on a napkin before answering. "Nope."

"Girlfriend?" Joe followed up.

"Not one of those either," Nash simply stated. In his opinion, it wasn't anyone's business who he slept with as long as he didn't lie about it.

By the time the impromptu party broke up it was nearly nine o'clock and Nash had started to really feel the alcohol buzzing through his system. He considered asking one of the guys to drive him home, but figured he could make the short two mile trip easily enough if he stayed on the side roads.

* * * *

Sidney was dozing on the couch when the front door opening woke him. He opened his eyes and wiped the drool from the corner of his mouth. "Hey."

Nash stumbled towards the sofa, giving Sidney just enough time to lift his legs before his lover collapsed. "We won our game."

Sidney settled his feet in Nash's lap. "Congratulations." He nudged Nash's balls with his toes. "Did you have fun at the bar with your friends?"

Nash rested his head against the back of the couch. "They're good guys."

"Are you drunk?" Sidney asked. He sat up and scooted over next to Nash.

"A little," Nash mumbled.

Watching Nash, Sidney couldn't believe what he was seeing. As far as he knew, Nash didn't get drunk. The times they'd gone out since moving to the Chicago area, Sidney had considered it a wild night if Nash had two drinks. He ran a finger down Nash's cheek. "Are you falling asleep?"

"Maybe."

Sidney exhaled his disappointment. He'd hoped to spend some time with Nash, but he could tell it wasn't going to happen. "Come on, let's get you to bed." He stood and tried to pull Nash to his feet.

It took several tries, but eventually Nash stood and let Sidney guide him towards the staircase in the small town house they'd leased. Once Nash had his hand on the banister, the journey went a lot smoother.

"I'll go lock up," Sidney said after getting Nash into the bedroom.

After locking the front door, Sidney went into the kitchen. He'd stopped at Nash's favourite deli on the way home from the construction site and picked up a couple of spicy Italian subs. He'd also stopped and picked up *The Wall Street Journal*. Sidney still didn't understand it, but Nash loved to lie in bed every Sunday and pore over the stock pages. The first time he'd seen Nash's nose buried in the stuffy newspaper he'd laughed. It was only the confused, hurt expression on Nash's face that had stopped Sidney from making a joke. He'd quickly learned to indulge his lover's odd curiosity about the stock market. Nash's sandwich went into the fridge before Sidney carried his to the small table. He unwrapped the white butcher paper and removed half of the footlong.

Although it wasn't the evening he'd hoped for, Sidney didn't begrudge Nash a night out with his new work friends. The move to Lake Forest hadn't been easy for Nash, but rarely, if ever, did he complain.

Sidney knew he was lucky to have Nash in his life. Since they'd relocated, Sidney had spent a lot of time working on the big library project. The design was still intact, but Sidney had been forced to make quite a few changes to accommodate the plot of land the county had purchased.

Once he'd finished his half sandwich, Sidney wrapped up the remainder and set it in the refrigerator next to Nash's. He took a few moments to put a load of jeans in the washer before turning out the lights and heading upstairs.

By the time he reached the bedroom, Nash was sound asleep. He cringed at the thought of Nash getting between the nice clean sheets without showering off the sweat and dirt that went hand in hand with playing softball.

Resigned to washing the sheets in the morning, Sidney undressed. He relieved himself and brushed his teeth before turning off the bedside lamp. Under the cover, Sidney moved over to curl around Nash. Clean or dirty, he wouldn't be able to sleep without holding on to his favourite security blanket.

"I love you," he whispered. He gave Nash a kiss on the cheek before settling down for the night.

* * * *

"Hey, kid," Bruce the contractor said over the walkie-talkie. "Would you come out here and look at something?"

Sidney ground his teeth. It didn't seem to matter how much work he put in at the job site, the construction crew continued to treat him like just another day labourer. He found his clipboard buried under a pile of schematics and walked out of the construction trailer into the scorching heat of a sunny August afternoon. He got to the bottom of the trailer steps before realising he hadn't thought to grab the hard hat Bruce insisted everyone wear.

After a quick trip inside to retrieve the fluorescent orange hard hat, Sidney strode towards the building. As he passed members of Bruce's crew, he was once again reminded of his place at the site. Where other workers wore the customary yellow hats, Bruce had given the orange one to Sidney his first day on site saying it would be the safest way for the rest of the guys to watch out for him.

He joined Bruce and Carl, one of the foremen. "What's up?"

Bruce pointed towards the blueprint attached to a sheet of lumber. "I think you screwed up on these footings," he said, tapping the drawing with his big sausage finger.

Sidney leaned over the drawing. "No I didn't. These are support footings for the archway."

Bruce shook his head. "I don't think they're necessary. The load should be fine without them."

Sidney took a deep breath. He'd tried to get along with Bruce, but the man refused to listen to Sidney on anything. "Sorry, but you're wrong. According to my calculations the weight of the arch requires the additional footings. If you don't have them in place now and something happens later, it'll cost a fortune to go back and fix the problem."

"Look, kid, I've done this longer than you've been alive, and I can tell you the added expense of the footings isn't necessary in this situation."

In Sidney's opinion, the integrity of the columns would be compromised. The last thing he wanted was to attach his name to a building that was structurally unsound. "I don't agree."

"Call your boss and get him out here," Bruce instructed. "Maybe I can have an intelligent conversation with someone *over* the age of thirty," Bruce mumbled under his breath.

Sidney strode back to the trailer, cussing Bruce the entire way. He smiled as he passed a few men who were part of the foundation crew, and received disgusted sneers from all five men in return.

"Go back to your cushy office, fairy boy," one of the men yelled to his back.

Sidney felt like taking off at a run, but tried to play it cool. He climbed the steps and shut himself in the relative safety of the ten by forty foot trailer. Ripping off the hard hat, he threw it across the small office and picked up the phone. They were in the beginning stages of the project. How in the hell was Sidney going to put up with the abuse for another year?

* * * *

By the time Sidney dragged his leather messenger bag up the front steps, he was beyond grouchy. Not only had he been talked down to by Bruce, but Harold Armstrong, Sidney's boss, had actually questioned Sidney on whether or not he was up to the challenge of working with real men.

Not knowing if the question had been in reference to his sexuality, Sidney had done the only thing he'd thought he could. He'd assured his boss he could handle Bruce and the other men on the construction site.

Sidney had hoped to make a few friends at work like Nash had done, but all the guys on the building site seemed to see was his slight frame and long hair. They knew nothing of his sexual preference but had taken to using the word 'fairy' to describe him.

He ran his hand over his newly-shorn head of hair. Telling Nash he'd done it so the other guys would stop giving him a hard time wouldn't work. No doubt Nash would storm down to the building site and try to take care of it, making Sidney look like even more of a kid.

Before he could come up with a way to explain his new haircut, the front door opened and Nash emerged. "What're you doing standing…?" Nash stopped and stared at Sidney for several moments. "What the fuck happened to your hair?"

Sidney fingered the buzzed sides of his head. He'd left the top a little longer to help hide his scars, but he had no doubt it was an abrupt change for Nash. "I need people to take me seriously." *Where the hell did that come from?* Sidney bit his tongue at the admission.

Nash pulled Sidney inside the town house and slammed the door. He set the puzzle book on the table. "Did something happen today, or have you been thinking about this for a while and just forgot to mention it to me?"

"It's my hair," Sidney said in a defensive tone. "If I want to cut it, I'll cut it."

Instead of firing back at him like Sidney expected, Nash pulled him into a hug. "Of course it is." He kissed the top of Sidney's head. "Just surprised me."

Understanding Nash was a hell of a lot harder to take than pissed off Nash at times. "It makes me look older," Sidney mumbled against Nash's shoulder.

"You're right. I was being selfish. I'm sorry." Nash continued to hold Sidney. "Hungry?"

"Starving."

"I bought stuff for chicken fried steak. Sound okay?"

Sidney nodded. "Sounds wonderful." The longer Sidney stayed in Nash's arms, the better he felt. What did he care if Bruce didn't respect him? In the end Sidney had won the argument about the footings. Isn't that all that should matter?

"Why don't you go take a shower while I start dinner?"

"It's my night to cook," Sidney reminded him. "Just give me a few minutes to wash my face and change my clothes."

Sidney started to pull away, but Nash held him in place. "I had a relatively easy day, but something tells me you didn't. I'll take care of dinner. You go get that shower."

Sidney smiled up at Nash. "You just want me to save my energy for after dinner."

"You bet your sweet ass I do."

Nash watched Sidney climb the steps and disappear from view. "Damn it," he said under his breath. He'd known it would make or break Sidney when he was told the company wanted him to oversee his award winning project, but Nash had hoped it wouldn't happen so fast.

He strode into the kitchen to start dinner, trying to control his anger. The architectural company had no business thrusting a recent graduate into a position like that, but when he'd raised his objections Sidney had assured him it would be good experience. Nash had seen Sidney's point at the time, but that was before the man he loved walked through the door with short hair.

It wasn't the length of Sidney's hair that pissed Nash off. Sidney was right, it was his hair, but Nash knew how much Sidney had loved it. Something major must have happened to make Sidney feel he needed to cut it.

Nash pulled the cube steak out of the refrigerator. He poured a good amount of flour on to a plate and seasoned it with salt and pepper before covering the steak in the mixture.

As the shortening melted in the frying pan, Nash started on the potatoes. Normally he'd make real mashed potatoes but he went with the instant this time. Once they were covered with good milk gravy made from the steak drippings Sidney probably wouldn't recognise the difference anyway.

He heard the shower shut off while he was in the middle of preparing frozen corn. Maybe he could get Sidney to open up about work. He doubted he could solve Sidney's problems at the building site, but at least he could try to be supportive. A thought suddenly hit him. What if the men from the construction site were responding to the obvious scar on Sidney's face and not his hair? He hated to think grown men could be that cruel, but he'd seen the way strangers tended to stare at Sidney when they were in public.

Nash grabbed a beer and the half gallon of milk out of the fridge. He drank close to a third of the bottle in one long gulp. Nash reckoned he deserved a beer since he'd declined Butch's offer to join a few of the guys at Wally's after work. Instead he'd gone grocery shopping to fill the void until Sidney got home.

One thing Nash still couldn't adjust to was all the downtime in his day. He was used to waking up with the sun and working late into the evening. It was between the hours of four-thirty, when he got off work, and around seven, when Sidney returned home, that he felt especially at a loose end. He'd even considered trying to find a part-time job to fill his day. He loved working brain teasers and crossword puzzles, but there were only so many games he could play. More often than not, he ended up at Wally's with the single men from work.

Despite his time at Wally's, Nash always tried to make sure he was home before Sidney. The arrangement seemed okay to Sidney because he rarely said anything about beer on Nash's breath.

"Man, I feel better," Sidney said, coming into the kitchen.

"Almost ready." After making sure the flour was browned in the frying pan drippings, Nash poured in the milk. "Would you mind setting the table?"

Sidney wrapped his arms around Nash's waist and gave him a hug. "Thanks for cooking."

"You know I don't mind," Nash said, reaching back to squeeze Sidney's ass. "Feel like talking about your day?"

"Not really." Sidney pulled away and started setting the table. He picked up Nash's beer and took a drink. "You want more of this with your dinner or something else?"

"I'll have iced tea and save the beer for this evening," Nash replied. He poured the gravy into a bowl and set it on the table. "Salt and pepper?"

"Yeah, I got it," Sidney said, joining Nash at the table.

Nash subtly tried to study Sidney as he filled his plate. "You were right about the haircut. It makes you look older."

"Good to know," Sidney mumbled around a bite of mashed potatoes. "Does it make me look like less of a fairy?"

Nash set down his fork and leaned his forearms on the table. "Who's calling you a fairy?"

"Who isn't?" Sidney tilted his head to the side until a loud crack sounded.

"Have you filed a complaint against them?" Normally Nash would never suggest such a thing, but Sidney was no match for a construction worker. If he couldn't use brawn to intimidate the men, perhaps he'd need to discuss the harassment with the company he worked for.

"No." Sidney took a deep breath and let it out slowly. "This is my first job. I can't start off my career by threatening people. I just need to figure out a way to handle it."

Nash reached across the table and ran his hand over Sidney's short wet hair. "Changing who you are in an effort to get them to accept you isn't the answer."

Sidney shrugged. "It's just hair."

"Sure," Nash said, dropping his hand. He realised he'd done the same thing with the guys at the garage. Not only had he not told them about Sidney, but he'd actually begun to laugh at their off-colour jokes just to fit in.

Standing, Nash crossed the small kitchen and pulled another beer out of the refrigerator. He sat back down and noticed Sidney's raised eyebrows. "Changed my mind."

"Okay."

Nash gestured to Sidney's plate. "Eat before it gets cold." He didn't want to delve any deeper into why he was willing to pretend he was someone else for a group of men who probably wouldn't have anything to do with him if they knew the truth.

Chapter Two

November 1990

Josh hugged Sidney outside the airport security gate. "It's good to see you again."

Sidney closed his eyes and squeezed Josh tighter. "I've missed you." Although he'd spoken on the phone to Josh at least once a month there was nothing like looking his friend in the eyes, too bad those eyes were currently bloodshot. Sidney wondered if Josh was weary from being on the road so long, or if his friend had enjoyed a joint before picking them up. He wanted to ask, but his relationship with Josh was finally beginning to improve. The last thing he wanted was to start lecturing Josh and lose what ground he'd gained. He released his hold and took a step back. "You look good."

Josh shrugged. "Looks can be deceiving."

Sidney noticed Josh's gaze going to the scar on his face. The scrutiny hurt, but before Sidney could question his friend, Nash stepped in and shook Josh's hand. "Tommy said you spent a few weeks at the ranch."

"Yeah, I passed through Kansas last month."

"How does it look?" Nash asked, leading the way towards the luggage carousel. Although Josh had returned to college he'd quit again after the first few weeks of classes. He'd spent the rest of the year travelling from place to place.

"Good, I guess. It was my first time there, so I don't really have anything to compare it with." Josh slung an arm around Sidney's neck. "Tommy gave me a couple bucks to clean out the stalls while I was there. Thank God, because I was nearly broke."

From buying weed, no doubt, Sidney thought. He reached for Nash's hand as they joined the rest of the passengers waiting for their luggage. It didn't sound as though Josh was any closer to getting his life back on track following the accident. "And Luke? How's he doing in school?"

Josh snorted. "Good, I guess. He brought someone home with him."

"A boyfriend?" Sidney indicated his suitcase and watched as Nash easily lifted it from the conveyor belt.

"I walked in on them making out, so I guess so. Although he introduced Brian as a friend."

"It's still all pretty new for him so cut him some slack," Sidney said, coming to Luke's defence.

"That's all of it," Nash said, pulling the handle up on his suitcase.

Josh led the way to the parking lot. Sidney was surprised to see an old, rust-eaten conversion van. It was obvious when Josh opened the door that he'd been living in it. Sidney bit his bottom lip.

"I'll ride back here," Sidney said, climbing in. He sat on the edge of the sheetless mattress and gritted his teeth.

"Sorry about that." It took several attempts, but eventually the van sputtered to life. "Mom's washing the sheets."

"I'm fine," Sidney said, meeting Josh's gaze in the rear-view mirror. He subtly rubbed his stomach. Inside he wasn't fine. It was another reminder of the accident that had changed their lives. While he'd tried to go on, and Luke was obviously doing well, Josh was slipping further and further away.

Never would Sidney have pictured the Josh he'd roomed with in college as the man driving towards the Ballentine house. He'd hoped the break from college and taking care of Luke would help heal Josh, but it appeared Josh was sinking deeper into a pit of despair of his own making. It was Sidney who had been driving the car that night. Josh had been sound asleep in the backseat when they'd struck the deer. Yet it seemed Josh was still carrying around a load of unnecessary guilt.

Sidney couldn't help but wonder whether or not it was guilt that was tearing Josh apart or something else. Hopefully he'd get a chance to have a heart to heart with his friend before the long Thanksgiving weekend was over.

Josh pulled into the circular drive in front of the Ballentine home and shut off the engine. The motor continued to sputter and spit for a few moments before eventually falling silent. He honked the horn and, before Sidney had a chance to climb out of the back of the van, the whole Ballentine family came pouring out of the house.

Josh's mother, Maggie, was the first to wrap her arms around Sidney. "It's so good to have you here again."

Sidney hugged back. Maggie was the closest thing he'd had to a mother since his own mom had passed away when he was a boy. "I've missed you," he said, kissing her cheek.

A round of handshakes followed. Each of the Ballentine brothers, along with Alan, the patriarch of the family, gave Sidney a warm and enthusiastic greeting. At the end of the line sat Luke. Although still thinner than before the accident, Luke looked damn good—happy. Sidney blinked several times as the sting of tears began. He shook his head and approached Luke.

Luke reached up and pulled Sidney down into a hug. "No crying. I'm good."

Sidney nodded, his face buried against Luke's neck. "I know. That's why I can't seem to keep the tears at bay." He distanced himself enough to stare into Luke's eyes. "You look happier than I've ever seen you." He stood straight and smiled at the man standing on the other side of the wheelchair. "I assume you have something to do with that."

Before reaching out to shake Sidney's hand, Brian glanced nervously around at Luke's family. "It's nice to meet you."

Sidney stepped to the side, putting his back towards the rest of the Ballentines and mouthed the words, "Thank you."

A blush crept up Brian's neck and face. Luke noticed the exchange and cleared his throat. "Well, someone grab the luggage and let's get out of this cold."

"Do you mind?" Sidney asked, moving to stand behind the wheelchair.

"I can do it," Luke answered.

"I have absolutely no doubt that you can do anything, but it'll get me out of carrying in the suitcases."

Luke laughed. "In that case, push away. I warn you though; a tiny fella like you'll have to get a running start to get me up the ramp."

Sidney sniffed. "I'm stronger than I look. I've been working out with Nash on the weekends."

The entire Ballentine clan plus Nash erupted in laughter. "Twice you worked out with me," Nash added.

Sidney took the laughter and the statement by Nash as a challenge. One way or another he would get Luke up the steeper than usual ramp or die trying. The first third of the concrete ramp wasn't a problem but then gravity kicked in. Sidney's muscles began to shake as he strained with all his might to get the wheelchair to the top.

Once he'd made it safely on to the porch, the obnoxious crowd behind him clapped. *Fuckers.* He played it off by turning around and sticking his tongue out at them, but at that moment his feelings hurt more than his muscles.

* * * *

Sidney woke after a short nap to find himself tucked under Nash's arm. When Nash had joined him on the couch Sidney didn't know. "What happened to the movie I was watching?" he asked around a yawn.

"It's been over for a while," Nash said. "Why don't you go on up to bed?"

Sidney sat up and rubbed the sleep from his eyes with the heels of his hands. "Is there any of that pie left?"

From his recliner, Alan turned away from whatever crime drama he seemed glued to. "Maggie made enough pies to last until next week."

Sidney stood, biting the inside of his cheek as his sore muscles protested the movement. "Good to know." He stepped over Nash's long legs and headed for the kitchen. It wasn't even Thanksgiving yet and already he'd probably gained a couple of pounds.

He found Maggie at the kitchen table playing cards with Brian, Luke and Eric. "Mind if I steal another piece of pie?"

Maggie set down her cards. "I'll get it."

Sidney reached her in time and applied pressure to her shoulders until she sat back down. "Please don't treat me like a guest."

Eric laughed. "In that case, the trash needs to be taken out."

Maggie reached over and slapped Eric's arm. "Hush. That's your chore and you know it."

"It's been my job since I was seven years old. What do you guys do when I'm away at school?" Eric asked.

"We pile it in the corner and wait with bated breath for your return," Maggie said without looking up from her cards.

"It's nice to see nothing's changed around here," Sidney said, grabbing a paper plate.

"Well, I'm out," Luke said, tossing his cards on to the table. "Would you mind making me one of those?" he asked Sidney.

"Not at all." Sidney retrieved another plate and added a slice of cherry pie. He started to set it down in front of Luke, but Luke stopped him.

"Why don't we eat in the sunroom?"

Sidney carried the plates into the window-filled room and put them on the small bistro table, making sure to move one of the chairs to the side. "You want a glass of milk?"

"Absolutely."

Sidney went back into the kitchen and filled two glasses with ice cold milk. He set them on the table and lowered himself in to the chair, wincing as his muscles protested once again.

"Sore?" Luke asked around a bite of pie.

"Yeah," he mumbled. "But don't spread that around."

"I won't." Luke took a drink and glanced at Sidney. "Have you talked to Josh?"

Sidney shook his head. "Just on the drive over from the airport. You?"

"No." Luke lifted another bite to his mouth. "It seems the more I try to get on with my life, the further away he slips from all of us."

"Yeah. I was thinking the same thing." Sidney tapped a cherry several times before spearing it with his fork. "Do you think he's doing drugs?"

Luke stared at his plate.

"Luke?" Sidney asked again.

It took several moments for Luke to answer. "I used to run out of pain pills before I should've when Josh took care of me. When I'd ask him about it, he'd get mad and tell me it was me who was taking too many. It just became easier to look the other way. When Josh suggested he needed to get away for a while, I hoped he'd pull himself out of it."

The sunny expression he'd witnessed on Luke's face all afternoon was gone. Sidney scooted his chair around the table to sit next to Luke. He reached out and took his friend's hand in his. "Don't let him pull you down with him. Let me talk to him. Maybe I can get him to step back far enough to see what his life's become."

Luke's eyes filled with tears. "What's happened to him? Why does he feel so guilty?"

"I don't know," Sidney said, squeezing Luke's hand. "But you have to promise me that, no matter what happens with Josh, you'll continue the path you're forging for yourself. Brian seems like a great guy."

"He is." Luke rubbed the tears from his eyes. "Can I tell you a secret?"

Sidney chuckled at Luke's devilish grin. "Sure."

"Brian isn't in college. He's my physical therapist, but he doesn't want anyone to know." Luke leaned as far forward as he could towards Sidney. "He tells me he loves the way I suck his cock." As soon as he'd said it, Luke's face turned bright red. "God, I can't believe I just told you that."

Sidney chuckled and released Luke's hand. "Does he make you feel good, too?" Sidney didn't know whether or not Luke had any feeling below the waist and it wasn't his place to ask, but he did want to make sure Luke wasn't just being used.

"His kisses…" Luke closed his eyes and groaned. "No offence, but that kiss we shared was nothing compared to Brian's."

"I'm glad. That's the way it should be." It hadn't answered his question, but at least Luke seemed happy with whatever physical pleasure Brian was able to give. "I think we both know the two of us wouldn't have worked anyway. I was trying to prove I could fall for someone other than Nash and you were just happy to be around another gay man."

"Yeah," Luke agreed. "I figured that out the first time I saw you and Nash together. It was always him, wasn't it?"

"Always."

* * * *

Nash woke with his cock poised at Sidney's hole. Whether he'd done it in his sleep or Sidney had put it there, he didn't know. "You awake?"

"Mmm hmm." Sidney wiggled his ass. "The smell of roasting turkey is making me horny."

Nash laughed. "You're sick. What, you got a thing for birds now?"

"Ewww, you're the sick one," Sidney said, elbowing Nash in the ribs. "The smell just reminds me that I'm in a home surrounded by the people I love. I think the horny part is just a by-product."

"Lucky me." Nash reached between them and began to rub the head of his cock up and down Sidney's ass crack. He wasn't a bit surprised that Sidney had already taken care of lubing his hole. His little sunshine never had the patience for long stretches of foreplay. "I don't smell turkey," he said, pushing the crown of his length inside Sidney.

"Really?" Sidney asked around a moan. "Wishful thinking, I guess." He pushed back, impaling himself on Nash's cock.

Nash reached for Sidney's leg to pull it farther out of the way, but a hiss from Sidney stopped him. "Sore?" Despite Sidney putting on a brave face the previous afternoon, Nash knew pushing Luke up the ramp had taken its toll.

"A little," Sidney admitted.

Nash rested his chin on Sidney's shoulder. "You know you have nothing to prove with these people, right? They don't give a shit how strong you are."

"I'm a man. I should be able to push my friend's wheelchair up a stupid ramp," Sidney spat. He moved, grinding against Nash's cock. "Fuck me," he growled.

Biting his tongue, Nash began to give Sidney what he'd asked for. When Sidney wanted to shut a conversation down or just get completely out of his head for a while, he craved hard, fast sex. At first the realisation that any cock would probably do when Sidney got that way hurt, but Nash didn't want Sidney to ever figure that out. He always wanted to be the man Sidney turned to when life became too much for him to handle.

So, Nash fucked Sidney as hard and fast as the bed and Sidney's sore muscles would allow. He didn't know why they continued to join the Ballentines for Thanksgiving. It seemed to take it out of Sidney to be around Josh and Luke.

Nash thought it had a lot to do with the Ballentine family as a whole rather than one or two individual members. Sidney seemed to crave the atmosphere created by the loving parents. It had been over six months since they'd heard from Jackson. Sidney's father seemed content to raise his new family and forget the old one. Although Sidney never mentioned it, Nash knew the snub hurt. Jackson might be an asshole, but he was still Sidney's father.

"Touch me," Sidney said, interrupting Nash's thoughts.

Nash relinquished his grip on Sidney's hip to encircle his cock. "This what you want?" he whispered in Sidney's ear as he began jacking him off. "You wanna come?"

"Uh huh." Sidney bucked back and forth between Nash's hand and cock.

Pressing his thumb under the crown of Sidney's dick, Nash was rewarded with the first spurt of seed. "Yeah, babe, come for me," Nash whispered, searching for his own release. He closed his eyes and imagined the two of them in a passionate embrace, tongues fighting for dominance.

Nash had changed since his years of fucking Reece just for the sexual release. He now craved the intimacy only being with Sidney provided. Love was as much a part of sex as the physical act itself. Sidney may need to get out of his head for a hard fuck on occasion, but the act itself wasn't enough for Nash anymore. "Love you," he whispered when he eventually fantasised his way to climax.

* * * *

Sidney caught Nash coming out of the kitchen, *The Wall Street Journal* tucked under his arm. He rolled his eyes and wrapped his arms around Sidney. Although Nash hadn't said anything about it, Sidney knew he'd hurt his feelings that morning. "Did you get enough to eat?"

"Too much," Nash answered before bending down for a quick kiss. "I offered to help Maggie with the dishes, but she threw me out of the kitchen."

"Why don't you go play stockbroker while I trick Maggie into letting me help?" Sidney stared up at Nash. He hated the worry lines that had begun to appear over the previous several months. Reaching up, Sidney ran his thumb over the deepening wrinkles on Nash's forehead. "You're my world. Don't ever doubt that."

Nash opened his mouth, but quickly closed it, obviously cutting himself off. He smiled down at Sidney. "I don't," he finally answered. He released his hold on Sidney and took a step back. "You'd better get in there before Maggie finishes."

Sidney nodded, holding Nash's hand until the last possible second as the man headed towards the family room. He waited until Nash had disappeared before stepping into the kitchen.

Maggie was humming to herself as she carefully washed the traditional china used for every Thanksgiving.

"You know, someday you're going to realise it's not the dishes that make Thanksgiving special," he said, grabbing a clean dish cloth from the drawer.

Maggie handed Sidney a freshly rinsed plate. "Tradition is important to Alan, so it's important to me."

Sidney dried the plate and set it to the side before reaching for another from the drying rack. "Are you trying to tell me you love Alan so much you're happy to stand in the kitchen alone for an hour after a meal just to wash dishes?"

"I'm saying, if eating on dishes once owned by his mother makes the man I love happy then I'll gladly wash them until the day I die." Maggie ran a finger over the filigreed edge of the plate. "How's Nash doing with the move?" she asked, changing the subject.

"Okay, I guess. He's found a group of friends he enjoys going out with after work." Sidney didn't mention the increasing amounts of alcohol Nash seemed to consume lately.

"Are they nice?"

"I don't know. I haven't met them," he confided.

"Why not?"

Sidney shrugged. "He doesn't want me to, I guess. He's never invited me to join them anyway."

Maggie turned her attention back to the dishwater, but not before Sidney saw the frown on her beautifully ageing face. "And what about you? Have you made any new friends?"

"No," he was quick to say. "I have Nash. That should be enough, right?"

"I love Alan with everything I am, but I still need a life outside our marriage. I have friends, Alan has friends, and we have a small group of friends we enjoy as a couple."

Sidney couldn't look at Maggie. He continued drying dishes for several moments. "I work with a bunch of butch construction guys who aren't interested in being my friend," he finally mumbled.

"What about getting to know some of the people who work for the same architectural firm?"

Sidney picked up the stack of plates. "I'm not in the office much, but maybe with winter coming..." He carried the plates into the formal dining room and began to put them away. How had the conversation got away from him? He'd wanted to discuss Josh, not his own personal problems.

At least he felt better about Nash's new friends. Maggie was probably right. Nash should have a group of friends that didn't include him. After all, it wasn't Nash's fault Sidney couldn't find any friends of his own.

Movement outside the window caught his attention. Josh was in the driveway cleaning out his van. Did he plan on leaving soon?

Sidney closed the china cabinet and sneaked out through the set of French doors. "It's kinda cold out here to be doing that today," he said, walking up on his friend.

"I thought I'd take off first thing in the morning," Josh replied, stretching a clean sheet over the mattress.

"Why?"

"It's just best that I do," Josh mumbled. He still hadn't turned to face Sidney, almost like he was hiding something.

Sidney climbed into the van and shut the door against the cold November air. "What's going on? I thought time away was supposed to help, but it's just made things worse. Why?"

Despite wearing his heavy boots, Josh crawled up on the mattress in an obvious attempt to put distance between them. "Go back inside. You're only going to make things worse."

"Worse? Is that possible?" Once Josh finally made eye contact, Sidney realised his friend was stoned. "What're you on?"

"Excuse me?"

Sidney moved from the space between the front seats to sit on the edge of the mattress. "You're high. Is that why you need to leave? You outta drugs?"

"Well, aren't you all high and mighty. I can remember a time when you were happy to get stoned with me."

"That was a long time ago. I've grown up a lot since then. Why haven't you?"

"Fuck you!" Josh spat. "You show up without a care in the world, parading that man of yours around like some prize. Last year you had, what, ten minutes to spare to talk to me? And then it was to yell at me, make me feel like shit on your shoes."

"That's not true. You avoided me because of this." Sidney pointed towards the disfiguring scar on his face. "You couldn't even stand to look at me." Sidney shook his head. "I'm not the one with the problem, you are."

Without warning, Josh launched himself across the mattress. Sidney closed his eyes, expecting a blow to the face. What he received instead was a set of cold lips pressed against his. Sidney's eyes popped open in shock. He tried to pull away, but Josh held the back of his head.

"Stop!" Sidney managed to say, his lips still pressed against Josh's mouth.

Josh released his hold on Sidney and sat back on his heels. His eyebrows drew together and the corners of his mouth turned downward. "Why didn't that feel good?" he whispered.

Sidney wasn't sure whether to be furious or sad at the bewildered expression on Josh's face. "Because it was one-sided." God, Sidney hated the lost look in Josh's eyes. "Are you gay?"

"No."

"Then why did you kiss me?"

"Because I watched you kiss Luke that night and it made me hard. So I thought…" Josh rubbed his eyes and backed away. "I saw the deer before you did."

"What? I thought you were out of it." Sidney moved to sit in the front passenger seat, reeling with questions. He stared out of the front windshield, waiting for Josh to say something.

"I…I don't know why I didn't warn you. I could tell that damn thing was getting ready to run out into the road," Josh managed to say seconds before a sob sounded.

Although there was the matter of Josh's reaction to the long ago kiss to address, Sidney knew Josh had just made one of the biggest confessions of his life. He took a deep breath before moving to join Josh on the bed. "Is that why you've practically destroyed yourself with guilt?"

Josh moved farther back on the mattress. "I could've prevented it, but I didn't want the kiss to end. How sick is that?"

"You couldn't have prevented it, Josh. If you'd yelled, it would've scared the shit out of me. The wreck could've been even worse than it was."

"How could it have been any worse? My brother will never walk again, and even though you try to pretend you don't look any different you do. Every time I see you or Luke I'm reminded that I didn't warn you that night."

The scar on Sidney's cheek began to tingle. Josh was right. He did pretend the scar was only visible to him. He'd somehow managed to convince himself the scar wasn't noticeable as long as he smiled. For a brief moment, he wondered if it was the reason he didn't have friends. He fingered the scar, lost in his own thoughts for several moments.

"I shouldn't have said that, I'm sorry. See? This is why I can't be around. I say and do shit I can't take back." Josh started to open the back door of the van.

Sidney threw himself across the length of the bed and wrapped his arms around Josh's chest before he could escape. He held his friend with all his strength, searching for the right words. "Don't go."

Josh's head lowered until his chin rested on his chest. Sidney loosened his hold but continued to hug Josh. "Are you addicted to pain killers?" he asked, resting his forehead on Josh's back.

"They help me forget."

"Forget? A shitty thing happened. You need to deal with it, not forget it."

"I thought if I kissed you, I'd understand, but I'm more confused than ever," Josh admitted.

"What do you need to understand? Why you got hard watching me kiss your brother?"

Josh nodded. "I loved you like a brother, but suddenly I opened my eyes to that kiss and something happened to me. I've seen that kiss over and over again in my dreams for years."

Sidney took a deep breath. "The kiss was intense. As drunk as you were that night, I'm not surprised it turned you on, but that doesn't mean you're gay or in love with me. Just means you're a horny bastard," he said, trying to lighten the mood.

Josh snorted. "I've fucked up our friendship, haven't I?"

"Nope. I've spent years waiting for you to get over your misplaced guilt. I never stopped hoping things could go back like they were before the accident, but that can't happen until you kick your habit and rejoin the land of the living."

"I've known for a while that I needed help, but my folks have been through enough."

Sidney ruffled Josh's hair. "Maggie hasn't said anything, but don't think for a second she doesn't know something's wrong. I imagine she and your dad would be more than happy to help if it meant getting their son back."

"Would you go with me to talk to them?" Josh asked.

"Only if you're serious about going into some kind of treatment programme." Sidney knew he had to be prepared to walk away from Josh if he reneged. He hated the thought of not visiting the Ballentines at Thanksgiving, but he knew he couldn't continue to spend the holiday fighting with Josh.

Josh nodded. "I am."

"Then let's go."

Chapter Three

April 1991

Carrying a plate of food to the table, Sidney straddled the birthday boy's lap. "I made all your favourites."

Nash settled his hands on Sidney's ass as Sidney lifted a sausage link to his mouth. "I thought you said I couldn't eat this stuff anymore," Nash said around the bite of food.

"According to your mom, you're not officially thirty-six until three-twenty this afternoon." Sidney licked a drip of savoury grease as it rolled down Nash's chin.

Nash nibbled the link to the nub before sucking the last bite, along with Sidney's fingers, into his mouth. "Mmm mmm."

Smiling, Sidney reached back to the table to retrieve a piece of bacon. It sucked that Nash's birthday had fallen on a Monday, but the two of them had celebrated the previous day. He couldn't believe Nash had actually worn the goofy party hat all day just to make Sidney happy. He had something special planned for after work, but wanted it to be a surprise. "I made reservations at Giovanni's for seven-thirty."

Nash nodded, his mouth full of food.

"Do you want your present now or then?" Sidney asked.

Nash ran his fingers down the seam of Sidney's cotton pants. "Depends on what it is."

With another piece of sausage at the ready, Sidney held it to Nash's lips. "That, my sweet man, is not something to be given only once a year. You pretty much have full access to my ass anytime you want it."

"Still a gift," Nash mumbled around Sidney's fingers.

With their time running short, Sidney couldn't contain his excitement. "Hang on." He climbed off Nash's lap and ran to grab his messenger bag out of the living room. Carrying it into the kitchen, he set it on the table before pulling out a large envelope. "Happy Birthday, Love."

Nash took the envelope and pulled Sidney back on to his lap. "You're too wound up for this to be a simple card."

Sidney nodded enthusiastically.

Nash opened the card and stared at the brochure and sizeable cheque inside. "I don't get it. Why're you giving me your bonus cheque?"

Sidney took the brochure and began to explain. "Well, I know you never got the chance to go to college, so I thought now might be the perfect time. I'm making enough to support us as long as we stay here in the town house."

"No. I'm not comfortable with you supporting me." Nash tried to hand the cheque back to Sidney.

Sidney quickly put his hands behind his back, refusing to accept the returned gift. "You gave up everything in order to come here with me. For nearly my entire life you've been the one person I could count on. Now that I'm able to give you something in return, let me. Go to school. Do something with your passion for numbers."

Nash shook his head and laid the cheque on the table. "I won't take payment for the things I've done for you." He lifted Sidney off his lap. "Now if you'll excuse me, I've got to get going before I'm late for work."

The rebuff hurt. Sidney stood, motionless, as Nash stormed out of the door. "What just happened?" he whispered to the empty room.

* * * *

"You gonna eat that?" Butch asked.

Nash pushed his untouched ham sandwich across the small lunch table. With his stomach still in knots, he knew there was no way he could keep it down. "Have at it."

Butch snatched the sandwich before Nash could change his mind. "What's up with you today? I thought birthdays were supposed to be happy occasions."

Nash glanced up from the table and narrowed his eyes. "How'd you know it was my birthday?"

Butch paused mid-bite. "Mac must've mentioned it."

What could Nash say to that? Mac was his boss and had access to personal information. "Just don't go spreading it around. I'm not really in a birthday mood today."

"Too late," Butch said around a mouthful of food. "We've already been talking about taking you out for a beer after work."

Nash thought of Sidney's plans for the evening. "Maybe a couple."

It wasn't that he didn't plan on making it home in time for their dinner reservation so what would it matter? Nash kept going over the morning's events. He'd been an asshole. No doubt about it, but the cheque had been a major blow to his pride.

He felt like Sidney was shoving money in his face while telling him he needed to improve himself by going to school. Nash stared at his hands. The grease seemed permanently embedded in each crack and groove. Did it embarrass Sidney to be seen in public with him? He thought of Sidney's clean soft hands. The man would never again have a callus and here Nash sat with nothing but. *Damn.*

* * * *

After leaving work at noon, Sidney gently sat the large sheet cake on the table. "Are you sure you don't mind me putting up a few decorations?"

"Go for it. I can't wait to see Nash's face when he walks in here," the bartender replied.

Sidney set to work standing on tables and fastening streamers to the ceiling. By the time he was finished, Wally's looked like a painted lady. His stomach rumbled, reminding Sidney he hadn't eaten. "Is the grill open?" he asked Kenny.

"Yeah, can I get you something?"

Knowing he and Nash had the same tastes in food, Sidney asked, "What's Nash usually order?"

"Cheddar burger with steak fries."

"Sounds good." Sidney sat on one of the stools at the bar while Kenny hollered the order to the cook. "I probably shouldn't start yet, but I could use a Coors Light."

"Draw or bottle?"

"Draw," Sidney answered. He glanced at the large bulletin board behind the bar. A familiar face was in several of the photographs. "You mind?" he asked, gesturing towards the pictures.

"Not at all."

Sidney stood and joined Kenny behind the bar to get a closer look. There were rows and rows of smiling men and women enjoying themselves. Nash's handsome face stood out more than the others, but perhaps it was because in each photograph Nash looked happier than Sidney had seen him in months. There were several group pictures with Nash front and centre, usually surrounded by more women than men.

"You have a lot of Nash," he commented.

"Yeah, the crew from Mac's are regulars. It seems whenever there's an occasion, those guys are smack dab in the middle of the fun."

Sidney swallowed around the lump in his throat. He'd had no idea Nash frequented the bar so often. Of course, by the time Sidney got off work and rode the Metra to Lake Forest it was usually close to eight before he was home. Sure, Nash usually smelt and tasted of beer, but Sidney assumed it was just a way for Nash to unwind.

Turning away from the pictures, Sidney went back to his stool and reached for the frosty mug of beer. It wasn't the fact that Nash hadn't told him about his regular trips to Wally's that bugged him most. It was the smiling face in the photographs that hurt.

"Nash seems to attract the ladies," he mumbled.

"That he does," Kenny confirmed.

No wonder Nash hadn't introduced Sidney to his friends: obviously his partner wasn't out of the closet. How far did Nash go with the women to pretend he was straight? Sidney remembered what Nash had told him about doing what he'd needed to do while in school to hide his homosexuality.

Sidney's hands started to shake. "Can I get that burger to go?"

"Sure."

He glanced over his shoulder at the decorations he'd spent several hours putting up. Would they embarrass Nash? Would he? Sidney suddenly felt like a fool for calling Mac and asking him to spread the word about a surprise party for Nash at Wally's. He hadn't explained his relationship with Nash other than to introduce himself.

Kenny sat a paper sack in front of Sidney. "There you go."

Sidney pulled a twenty out of his pocket along with an envelope of cash. He'd planned to pay for a keg of beer and just because he wouldn't be attending the party was no reason to let the others down. "This is for the keg."

"You can pay after the party," Kenny told him.

Sidney stood and shook his head. "I won't be here. Do me a favour and don't tell Nash who set up the party."

"There a reason you're not coming?"

Sidney glanced at the photographs once more. "Not in a party mood. Besides, he'll have a better time without me around. I just wanted to give him something he'd remember."

By the time he'd gathered his things and left the bar, Sidney felt gutted. He tried to remember what Maggie had said about Nash needing friends outside their relationship. Since Sidney had very few friends, he didn't know if Nash's actions were normal or not. What he did know was that he'd never have done the same thing to Nash. Sidney had always been beyond proud of his partner, and he'd thought Nash felt the same.

* * * *

Nash's jaw dropped when he walked into Wally's. "What the fuck is all this?"

Kenny held up his hands. "Don't look at me, I didn't do it."

"Hey, Birthday Boy, get over here and help us drink this pitcher," Butch called from their usual table.

Nash walked over and was promptly handed a beer. He stared down at the cake on the table and shook his head. Within moments the bad mood he'd carried around all day began to evaporate. He'd never had friends who had cared enough to throw him a party. Glancing around the table, Nash couldn't wipe the smile from his face. "This is great. Thanks."

"Drink up," Joe prompted, waving the pitcher around.

"I'll be right back. I need to use the restroom." Nash retreated to the restroom area and picked up the payphone. He was surprised when Sidney picked up on the third ring. "Hey, I didn't think you'd be home."

"It's your birthday," Sidney said.

Nash rubbed the back of his neck. "Yeah, well, would you mind if I had a couple of beers with the guys from work before I come home?"

"Something going on?"

Nash swallowed around the lump in his throat. "Not really. They just wanna buy me a few birthday drinks. I'll be home in time to make it to the restaurant though."

"Do what you want," Sidney mumbled.

Nash wondered if Sidney was still mad about the way he'd left that morning. "It's no big deal, just a couple of beers."

Sidney was quiet for several seconds. "If it's no big deal, don't worry about it."

Nash let out a loud, annoyed sigh. "Stop pouting. You're not a kid anymore."

"Whatever. I'll cancel the reservation. Have fun."

Before Nash could reply, Sidney hung up the phone. "Sonofabitch!" Nash growled, slamming the receiver back into its cradle. All he'd asked for was a couple of hours with friends, men who asked for nothing other than conversation and a good time. Friends who cared enough about him to buy him a Goddamned cake!

By the time Nash made it back to the table, he was beyond aggravated at Sidney for the way he'd acted. "Fill me up," he said, holding out his glass.

* * * *

It was after midnight when Sidney heard the front door slam shut. Several moments later he heard a loud thud then nothing. Throwing back the covers, Sidney grabbed his robe and crept down the stairs. "Nash?"

When he received no reply, he started to worry until he spotted his partner, half on, half off the couch. Nash appeared to be passed out. Sidney went to the front door and opened it. Nash's truck wasn't in the drive. "At least he didn't drive home drunk."

Sidney shut the door and locked it before turning out the lights. He didn't bother waking Nash. There was no way he could've got the drunken man up the steps anyway. He thought about getting a blanket out of the linen closet, but decided against it. "Let him suffer."

* * * *

Shielding his eyes against the bright sunlight streaming through the window, Nash tried to roll over and promptly fell to the floor with a thud. "What the hell?" he grumbled, grabbing his aching head.

It took him several seconds to figure out why he was sleeping on the couch. He didn't remember much of his ride home from Wally's other than Kenny putting him into a taxi. Nash ran his fingers through his hair, stopping to scratch his scalp. He still had his shoes on. Sidney had to have heard him come in and just left him where he was.

Struggling to his feet, Nash stumbled towards the small half bath on the main floor. As he relieved himself, he tried to remember details of the previous night. He'd been pissed at Sidney for acting like there was something wrong with him having a drink with his friends. Although he hadn't told Sidney about the party they'd thrown for him, all he'd asked for was a couple of hours before coming home.

Nash shook off and flushed the toilet before heading upstairs. Whatever the hell was wrong with Sidney, Nash would feel better if they could hash it out before work. Upon entering the bedroom, he stopped in his tracks.

Not only was the bed made, but there was no sign of Sidney. For the first time since he'd opened his eyes,

Nash glanced at the clock. "Fuck!" he yelled. He instantly regretted it as his head threatened to topple from his neck.

He was already an hour late for work. It was one thing to leave him on the couch all night, but the least Sidney could've done was wake him before he'd left for the construction site. No way would he have time for a shower. He just hoped Mac wouldn't mind him coming in smelling of cigarettes and beer.

* * * *

Sidney poured another cup of coffee, happy he was working in the office instead of being stuck out on the job site.

"Someone looks grouchy this morning," Bobbi said, holding her cup out.

The only reason Sidney proceeded to pour the woman's coffee was because he actually liked her. Besides him, Bobbi seemed to be the only other square peg in the firm. "Bad night."

Bobbi giggled. "Drink too much at Nash's party?"

She'd been the only one Sidney had told about his surprise gift for Nash. He'd almost invited her to come along. He was very glad he hadn't. "Didn't go."

Bobbi pulled Sidney over to the side of the break room in front of the floor to ceiling windows. "What do you mean you didn't go? What happened?"

Sidney was about to open up to the redhead when his boss walked into the room. "Drinks after work?"

"You're on," she said, a sparkle in her big blue eyes.

By the time he'd made it back to his desk, Sidney's mood was a tad lighter. He'd never gone out with a colleague after work, but if Nash could do it and not feel guilty, so could he.

* * * *

"Four-thirty, time to clock out," Butch said, coming up behind Nash to slap him on the back.

Nash grabbed the red shop rag out of his back pocket and wiped some of the grease from his hands. "I was late getting in this morning, so Mac said I could make it up."

Butch laughed. "Yeah, that was one hell of a party your friend threw you. What I couldn't understand is why he didn't come."

"What're you talking about? What friend?"

Butch shrugged and put on a pair of sunglasses. "No clue. All I know is some guy called Mac last Thursday and said to spread the word about your surprise party at Wally's. I assumed it was your boyfriend or something, but when he didn't show I figured I was wrong."

Nash's stomach dropped. His surprise must've shown on his face. Butch chuckled again. "Yeah, I figured it out a while back. Don't worry, your secret's safe."

"You're not mad?"

"Nah. I know not everyone in the shop would understand. As long as you don't start staring at my ass when I'm bent over an engine, we're cool."

"As if," Nash snorted, trying to cover his embarrassment.

"I'm outta here," Butch said, strolling out of the roll-up door towards his motorcycle.

Nash watched Butch drive off, still stunned. A quick glance at the clock told him he still had fifty minutes of time to make up before he could go home and talk to Sidney. If Sidney really had planned the surprise party, why hadn't he said anything? For that matter, why hadn't Sidney come? A thought hit him. What if Sidney knew Nash was in the closet at work?

"Shit," he spat, ducking back under the hood.

* * * *

Sidney met Bobbi in front of the high-rise where they both worked. He was surprised to see the woman quickly put out a cigarette. "You smoke?"

Bobbi bit her plump lower lip. "Ya caught me."

Sidney glanced around like a junky ready to score. "You got one for me?"

Bobbi's red eyebrows shot up to her hairline. "You smoke?"

"Used to," he said, lighting the cigarette. He put his back to the building and blew the smoke straight up. He swore he could feel the nicotine coursing through his veins after just one puff. "Nash made me quit."

"Then you're lucky. I've never had anyone who gave a shit if I smoked or not." Bobbi lit up another cigarette and joined Sidney with her back against the wall.

"I find that hard to believe. If that really is the case, my guess is that's the way you want it. Gay or not, I know an attractive woman when I see one."

Bobbi bumped her shoulder against Sidney's. "People have always considered me weird." She shrugged. "So be it. If having my own sense of style and a mind of my own makes me weird, I accept that."

Sidney glanced at Bobbi. There had to be more to the story, but it was too early in their tentative friendship to press. "So where do people go for a drink around here?"

"I don't give a flyin' flip about where people go. I like Maria Bella's. It's not hip or trendy, but their drinks are reasonable and people leave me the hell alone."

They finished their cigarettes and sunk the butts into the pot of sand housed nearby. "Which way?" Sidney asked.

Bobbi gestured with her head and took off down the sidewalk. He watched the way her peasant skirt blew around in the wind for several seconds before jogging to catch up to her. For a woman of around five-foot-two, Bobbi could eat her way down a sidewalk.

"Are you from Chicago?" Sidney asked.

Bobbi laughed. "Hardly. I was born and raised near Woodstock, New York." She peered over her black-cat glasses. "Before you ask, yes, my parents are as free-spirited as I am."

Sidney had a hard time trying to fit a person like Bobbi into the corporate world. "So why architecture?"

"Because if someone doesn't start caring about this planet we're all doomed. I truly believe solar panels are the way of the future, and if it takes a fantastically designed building to get customers to see that, so be it."

They turned the corner and made their way down one of the side streets. "I'd like to look at your designs sometime," Sidney commented.

"Careful what you ask for. I've been known to step up on my soapbox when explaining my work."

"That's fine with me. I get the same way with my work. When you're passionate about something it's hard not to want others to understand it."

Bobbi looped her arm around Sidney's. "I think this is the beginning of a great friendship."

* * * *

It was almost nine o'clock when Sidney arrived home. Nash had been beside himself with worry. Especially after he'd found the paper sack and food wrapper from Wally's in the trash can. Even worse, he'd only found it by digging through the trash looking for clues as to whether or not Sidney had planned and executed the party. The wrapper containing a half-eaten cheeseburger inside was proof of Sidney's involvement in the surprise party.

Sidney stopped suddenly in the process of removing his key from the lock. "Oh, you're home."

"Of course I'm home," Nash answered from his position on the couch. "Where've you been? I was worried when you didn't call or come straight home."

"I went out for a drink with a colleague from work." Sidney shut the door and locked it, tossing his keys onto the small table. He picked up the pile of mail and started looking through it, ignoring Nash.

"What friend from work?"

"Bobby," Sidney said, dropping the envelopes back onto the table. He passed Nash and strode towards the kitchen.

Nash jumped off the couch and followed Sidney. "Bobby who? I've never heard you talk about a friend named Bobby."

Sidney pulled a bag of corn chips out of the cabinet. "I don't think you want to go there with me, Nash. Not right now, anyway." Sidney grabbed a Coke out of the refrigerator and headed out of the room without even looking at Nash.

"Stop running away from me!" Nash yelled to Sidney's retreating back.

"I'm not *running* anywhere," Sidney answered. "I'm *walking* upstairs to watch TV."

"We need to talk about last night," Nash said, following Sidney up the steps.

"No. We really, really don't. If you want to continue to lie to your friends, be my guest, but I can promise you one thing. I will never." Sidney stopped on the top step and turned to stare at Nash. "Ever. Throw you a party again."

Nash sighed. "I'm sorry about that. I didn't know you were the one who'd done all that."

"Doesn't matter." Sidney walked into the bedroom and kicked off his shoes. He set the can of Coke and chips on the bedside table before disappearing into the bathroom.

"It matters to me," Nash said through the closed door.

When he received nothing in reply, Nash began to undress for bed. He'd already taken his shower, happy to get the stink from the previous night off him. In a last second decision, Nash left his underwear on and climbed under the covers, resting his back against the headboard.

When Sidney walked out of the bathroom wearing a pair of sleep pants, Nash knew he was in deep trouble. Never once since they'd got together had Sidney worn a stitch of clothing to bed.

Once again, Sidney ignored Nash as he turned on the television and grabbed the chips. "Would you turn that down so we can talk?" Nash asked.

With an exaggerated sigh, Sidney made a production of stabbing the mute button before crossing his arms. "Even if you didn't know I was the one behind the party, it would've been nice had you invited me to come down to the bar and join you. Of course that would mean acknowledging your queer side."

Sidney was right. There was no way Nash could argue the statement. "I'm sorry. It's just that the guys I work with aren't really open-minded when it comes to stuff like that."

"So why be friends with them?"

"Because maybe it sounds selfish, but my relationship with you is only part of who I am. Why can't I shut that part of myself off if it means feeling liked and accepted by the people I'm surrounded by every fucking day? I know you don't understand what it's like, but I grew up one of the popular kids. I guess I'm not ready to give that feeling up."

Moisture filled Sidney's eyes. "You're right. I don't know how that feels."

Nash reached for Sidney when he threw back the covers. "Wait. I'm sorry. I shouldn't have said that."

Sidney moved his arm, dislodging Nash's tentative hold. "Don't worry about it. The truth is the truth," he said, getting out of bed. Once again, Sidney disappeared into the bathroom and shut the door.

Nash thumped his head against the bed several times before getting up. He was prepared to find the door locked, so it was a surprise when it opened easily. Sidney sat on the closed toilet lid, his forearms resting on his thighs.

Nash knelt beside Sidney and rested his forehead against Sidney's knee. He needed to put into words what he'd been hiding from Sidney since their move to Lake Forest. "I felt so lonely before I made friends with the guys from the shop. I know it's not your fault, but you're never here. Back home it didn't bother me as much because I had other things to do, but there are no horses housed behind the town house."

"I come home to you every single night. And rarely do I get to kiss you anymore without tasting beer. I don't say anything because I know you go to the bar after work so you don't have to come home to an empty house. It's the reason I thought you'd be happy if I threw you a party with your friends. I just didn't realise at the time that I'm not one of them anymore."

"Don't say that," Nash said around the lump in his throat. He tilted Sidney's chin up so he could look into those gorgeous green eyes he'd fallen in love with. "You're my best friend. You'll always be that for me."

Once again, Sidney's eyes filled with tears. "Before today, you were my only friend here. How do you think it made me feel when I realised you'd rather spend your birthday with people who don't even know I exist?"

Nash pulled Sidney off the toilet and into his arms. "I'm a real sonofabitch, aren't I?"

Sidney remained quiet, in silent agreement evidently.

"Tell me about your new friend?" Nash asked, trying to tamp down his earlier jealousy.

"Bobbi, with an *i*, is a lot like me. Neither of us fit in with the others. For some reason I really needed to connect with someone today, so I invited her out for a drink after work."

"Her?" Nash asked, relieved.

Sidney nodded.-

"Were you planning on telling me your new friend is a woman?" He spotted a brief sparkle in Sidney's eyes and knew the answer. "Did you want me to be jealous?"

Sidney shrugged. "It'd be a nice change of pace." He moved his head back, away from Nash's hand, but didn't break eye contact. "I've been through a lot of shit in my life, but I can honestly say, yesterday was right up there with one of the worst days I've experienced."

Nash held Sidney tighter, needing the contact. "How can you say that? You almost lost your life in a car accident, not to mention your mom's death."

Sidney's Adam's apple bobbed several times. "Because it was the first day since you told me you loved me that I didn't feel it."

The answer hit Nash like a Mac Truck. "I'm sorry I made you feel that way. I know your schedule isn't your fault, but I think there's a part of me that wanted to make you pay for it anyway." He rested his forehead against Sidney's. "I only have two choices as far as the guys from work are concerned. I can either quit or stay in the closet. Although I did find out earlier that Butch knows the truth. Of course, he agreed with me on keeping my sexuality a secret from the others."

Sidney shook his head. "Believe it or not, I do understand that. It's not that that hurt me. It was the feeling that you'd rather be with them than me."

"It's going to take me a long time to make this up to you, isn't it?" Nash surmised.

"Probably."

"Can we compromise?" Nash asked.

"Hopefully."

"Why don't we pick a night during the week when it's okay to go out with our friends? The rest of the week can be reserved for just us." Nash bit his bottom lip. He really did enjoy hanging out with the guys, but nothing was worth alienating the man he loved.

"Friday nights," Sidney supplied. "That way we don't have to worry about going to work the next day."

"Deal." Nash knew he'd dodged a bullet, but he couldn't help but wonder how long the misunderstanding would plague their relationship.

Chapter Four

"What if no one shows up?"

Nash reached across the seat and grabbed Sidney's hand before he could bite his nails to the quick. "Are you kidding? The entire community's been waiting for this."

It was the day of the official ribbon-cutting ceremony at the library. Nash didn't doubt half the town would be on hand to get their first look inside the unique building. Although he hadn't told Sidney, Nash had driven by the project often, and he had no doubt the public would be wowed by the results.

Turning the corner, Nash's pickup came to a stop. Even though the library was still four blocks away, policemen were doing their best to direct traffic. With long lines in all directions, it seemed there weren't enough parking spaces in the entire town to accommodate the throngs of people. "Damn. Where'd all these people come from?"

Sidney unbuckled his seat belt and bent over, holding his head. "I think I'm gonna be sick."

Nash chuckled and rubbed Sidney's back. "You'll do fine."

"Remind me again, why did I agree to make a short speech?" Sidney groaned.

"Because this whole project was your baby. You deserve it. Just be grateful we have a reserved parking space pass."

They were eventually directed to the parking lot where the other officials were parked. According to Sidney, representatives from the county library board as well as state and local politicians would be on hand for the ceremony.

He climbed out of the truck and reached behind the seat for his suit jacket, the same one he'd worn to Sidney's graduation. It amazed him how far Sidney's career had come in such a short time. It was further proof of his partner's talent and dedication. "Ready?"

Sidney shook his head. "Give me a second."

Nash walked to the front of the truck and stared at the concrete and glass building. From the front, the two-storey library looked like six upright books. The artist the firm had hired had done an amazing job of painting the book spines. If Nash hadn't known better, he would have sworn the books were wrapped in colourful leather. The gilded titles of some of the most revered books in the world brought a smile to his face. "I'm glad they added *Charlotte's Web*. That was always one of my favourites."

"I know," Sidney said, joining him. "Mike did it as a favour to me. The rest of the books were chosen in a contest."

Nash wrapped an arm around Sidney. "Thank you."

Sidney glanced up at Nash and shook his head. "No. It's my way of thanking you. I wouldn't have accepted the job if you hadn't agreed to follow me here. I know I don't say it enough, but I'm grateful every day that you love me."

Nash bent down and gave Sidney a quick, soft kiss. "I'm grateful you let me."

"Oh my God, it's fantastic!" A woman with long red hair hanging in row after row of tiny braids and a bohemian-style dress ran towards them. Nash had no doubt it was Sidney's friend Bobbi.

Sidney pulled away from Nash and accepted Bobbi's enthusiastic hug. "Thanks."

Nash spotted a group of familiar faces. "Well, look what the cat dragged in."

Sidney released Bobbi. By the angry expression on Sidney's face, it was apparent he thought Nash was making a comment about Bobbi's appearance.

Nash pointed towards the group of people standing in the grass. Although he hadn't known they would actually show up, Nash had emailed Luke to tell him about the grand opening.

Sidney's face lit up. He grabbed Nash and Bobbi by the hand and pulled them towards the Ballentine family. Despite the fact that restraint was not one of Sidney's strong points, he managed to hold his joy intact until they crossed the parking lot. He released Nash's hand and all but ran towards the group of clapping friends. "I can't believe you're here!"

"It's your big day. How could we stay away?" Maggie asked, enveloping Sidney in a motherly hug. "I'm so proud of you."

A lump formed in Nash's throat as he watched the pair. He knew they were both thinking of Sidney's mother and wishing she could've lived to see the day.

Stepping forward, he reached out and shook Alan's hand before moving on to Luke. "You look better every time I see you."

Luke grinned. "That's not saying much, seeing as how the first time you saw me I was in a coma."

Brian, who stood just behind Luke, ruffled Luke's hair. "Behave." He held his hand out. "Good to see you again."

"Likewise," Nash said.

By the time Nash was finished shaking hands, Sidney had torn himself away from Maggie and was in the process of hugging Josh. For the first time in memory, Josh looked somewhat happy. Gone was the sour expression the man had seemed to constantly wear.

"He's doing so much better," Maggie said in Nash's ear. "He completed the programme and has been one hundred percent clean since December first."

Nash nodded, acknowledging the achievement, but he wasn't ready to forgive Josh for all the hurt he'd caused Sidney. "Good to hear."

Josh and Sidney were still huddled together talking, but, with time ticking away, Nash stepped over. "It's almost time," he reminded Sidney.

Sidney gave Nash a kiss on the cheek. "Do me a favour and introduce Bobbi to everyone."

"Will do." Nash gave Sidney another kiss. "Good luck."

"I'll need it," Sidney said with a chuckle. He waved to everyone as he hurried towards the podium set up in front of the library.

Although there were no doors or windows on the front of the building, the backdrop of the towering books was perfect. The entire back of the building was made of glass with a spectacular view of Lake

Michigan. Although pictures hadn't shown up yet in magazines or newspapers, Nash knew it was only a matter of time before Sidney's career exploded.

Nash hoped he was ready, but, as he stared up at the impressive building, he couldn't help but fear the years ahead. If Sidney became as sought after as Nash predicted, would there still be room for him?

* * * *

After an impromptu dinner party at a local restaurant, Nash helped Sidney up the front steps. "It would be easier for me to just carry you," Nash commented.

"I'm not that bad," Sidney said, leaning heavily against the rail.

"How much did you drink, anyway?"

Sidney laughed. "No idea. People just kept buying me drinks so I drank 'em."

Once they made it inside the town house, Nash led Sidney to the sofa. "Sit tight while I lock up."

Closing his eyes, Sidney sighed. "Not going anywhere."

Nash crossed through to the kitchen for pain relievers and a bottle of water. "Here," he said, joining Sidney on the couch.

While Sidney fumbled to take two of the pills from the jar, Nash removed his suit jacket. Hopefully it'd be another year before he had to wear the damn thing. He smiled to himself. It had all been worth it, though, to see and hear Sidney up on the podium. There had even been a writer from *Architectural Digest* on hand to interview him for an planned spotlight piece the magazine was doing on up and coming architects.

Free of his coat and tie, Nash pulled Sidney into his arms. "The library is spectacular. You should feel so proud of yourself."

Sidney began unbuttoning Nash's shirt, kissing his way down as he did. "If they put me in the article, I'd like to send a copy to Dad."

Nash blinked in surprise. Sidney rarely spoke of his father, but when he did it was usually something negative. "If that's what you want. Although I hope you know you don't have anything to prove to him."

Sidney slid to the floor and unfastened the top of Nash's pants. "I know I don't, but would it sound petty if I wanted to do it anyway?"

Nash ruffled Sidney's hair. "No. Just makes you human." He lifted his hips so Sidney could slide his pants down. There were few things in life he enjoyed more than having Sidney's lips wrapped around his cock, and, even though it was technically Sidney's day to shine, Nash didn't protest as his partner swallowed his length.

With his slacks bunched around his ankles, Nash tried to spread his legs as much as possible. Although he never asked for it, he secretly hoped Sidney's talented tongue would find its way to his ass.

Sidney nuzzled his face against the short curls surrounding Nash's cock. "Love the way you smell."

Nash rested his head against the back of the sofa and toed off his dress shoes. He could spend the rest of his life getting praised and loved by Sidney and never tire of it. Some men were horrible lays when they drank, but not Sidney. It seemed the more Sidney drank, the better their lovemaking. Nash assumed it had something to do with Sidney letting go of the pressures of his everyday life and just living in the moment.

Whatever it was that allowed Sidney to slow down and thoroughly enjoy himself, Nash was all for it. Sidney slowly licked and sucked Nash's cock from root to crown while his fingers began to explore the crack of Nash's ass. "Oh, yeah," he moaned when Sidney zeroed in on his hole.

Sidney released Nash's cock and grinned. "You like that, don't you?"

"I love that," Nash answered, pushing his pants off so he could rest his heels on the edge of the sofa.

"It's been a long time since I fucked you," Sidney whispered.

"It's your night. You can do anything to me you want." Nash rarely made the offer. Perhaps he'd had too many drinks, as well. Nash refused to examine the reason he was willing to give up complete control when Sidney's tongue began to lap at his asshole. "Right there. Oh, fuck!" he growled.

Sidney sat back on his heels and ran his palms up Nash's body to pinch his nipples. "Let's go upstairs."

"I'm pretty comfortable right here," Nash answered.

"But the lube's upstairs," Sidney grumbled.

"You could just go back to rimming," Nash offered.

"Not if you want me to last until I fuck you," Sidney countered.

Chuckling, Nash sat up. "You on a hair trigger?"

"Something like that." Sidney got to his feet and began stripping his clothes as he walked towards the staircase.

Nash watched Sidney shed his clothes and groaned. Although Sidney was still too thin, and probably always would be, his body had begun to attain definition. The lean muscles were sexy as hell on the golden boy of the architectural world.

Nash followed Sidney upstairs, his erection bobbing almost painfully with each step. He settled his hand around his length and entered the bedroom.

Sidney gestured to the bed before retrieving a blue scarf from the top dresser drawer. Nash couldn't help but chuckle as Sidney draped the sheer fabric over the bedside lamp, casting the room in a cool blue glow. The first time Sidney had draped the lamp, Nash had thought it was corny as hell, but he'd quickly warmed to the muted light. He positioned himself on his hands and knees and presented his ass to Sidney, asking without words for more of what he'd been given downstairs.

Before getting into bed, Sidney grabbed the bottle of lube from the drawer. "Tongue or fingers?" he asked, settling behind Nash.

"Both. Please, God, both," Nash practically begged.

Sidney playfully bit Nash's butt. "You have the best ass."

Normally Nash would refute the statement, but at the moment he just wanted Sidney's mouth, more specifically, his tongue. He bit his bottom lip, waiting, trying like hell to be patient. Then it happened. The tip of Sidney's tongue stabbed against Nash's hole, and Nash's body came alive.

Nash reached for his cock as Sidney began sucking and licking Nash's ass. Heaven was the only way to describe it. Maybe he needed to ask for it more often. He laid his head on the blanket so he could jack himself with one hand and try to hold his ass open with the other. It wasn't until he felt moisture run down his cheek that he realised he was drooling. *Sonofabitch!* Sidney had reduced him to a slobbering mess.

Sidney introduced a finger to Nash's relaxing hole. "Okay?"

"Uh huh," Nash managed to get out.

With the aid of warm spit, Sidney soon worked his way up to three fingers deep in Nash's ass. "So hungry," Sidney chuckled.

"Starved," Nash grunted. He heard the soft snick as Sidney opened the bottle of lube. "Love me," he mumbled, pressing his thumb against the underside of his cock.

"Always." Sidney removed his fingers and replaced them with the crown of his cock. "Don't clench up on me now," he warned.

Nash hadn't even realised he'd done it. He blew out several times, willing his body to return to its relaxed state. He turned his face to the mattress and scrunched his eyes closed as an uncomfortable pinch followed Sidney's entrance into his body.

"Okay?" Sidney asked.

Nash nodded, knowing the pain would soon subside and give way to the euphoric pleasure he was desperately reaching for. He wasn't sure why the two of them didn't swap places more often, except that Nash loved taking care of Sidney, and Sidney seemed to crave being taken care of. At least in bed, he mentally added.

Buried to the hilt, Sidney leant down and kissed Nash's spine. "I'd almost forgotten how good you feel wrapped around my cock," he whispered.

Once the pain subsided, Nash turned his head to gaze back at Sidney. "Love you," he mouthed.

"You too," Sidney replied, before starting a slow rhythm.

Nash let his mind wander as he gave himself over to the pleasure Sidney bestowed so freely. It hadn't been easy since moving to Chicago, but he knew he'd follow Sidney to the ends of the earth if he needed to.

Lulled by the slow fucking, Nash's body jerked when Sidney suddenly slammed deep and hard. He rose up on his arms and looked over his shoulder. Head tilted back and eyes closed, Sidney appeared to be in his own state of bliss. The fucking became steadily faster, making Sidney's breathing pick up. *Fuck, he's beautiful*, Nash thought, staring at the man he loved above all others.

It was that thought that prompted the first strand of seed to shoot from Nash's cock on to the blanket below. "Coming!" he howled.

"Right there," Sidney gasped, his face contorting with the intensity of his own orgasm.

Nash milked the last drop from his cock before collapsing on to the bed with Sidney landing with a thud on top of him. Nash fought to get his breathing under control while spots danced behind his closed eyelids. Nash didn't know if it was the exhaustion of the busy day combined with the perfect ending, or if his blood pressure had spiked again. He hadn't said a word to Sidney, but he'd had several brief moments of dizziness over the last few months.

Sidney rolled off Nash and cuddled against him. "Too tired to get up."

"Just sleep," Nash said, brushing Sidney's cheek.

* * * *

Sidney sat between Nash and Josh at the long table. It was the last time he'd see the Ballentines before they all boarded a plane to return to their lives in Pennsylvania. With Nash involved in a discussion with Peter, the stockbroker of the family, Sidney turned his attention to Josh.

Although the man had assured Sidney he was off the prescription pain pills, Sidney was anxious to talk about what Josh had planned for his future. "Given any more thought to finishing college?"

Josh took a sip of his orange juice. "A little. I was impressed by the counsellors at the treatment hospital, especially the ones who'd fought their own battles with drugs. I could see myself working there."

"That's great. You should go for it."

Josh nodded before eating another bite of his brunch. "What's the story with that friend of yours, Bobbi? She's hot," Josh said around a mouthful of food.

Sidney's protective instincts kicked in. As much as he still loved Josh, Sidney didn't want to introduce the possible heartache that tended to follow Josh around like a bad penny. Bobbi meant too much to him for that. Besides, she'd had more than her share of players float in and out of her life. Even though Sidney had no idea what Josh's sex life had encompassed since their college days, he remembered Josh going from girl to girl. Nope, not what Sidney wanted for Bobbi.

"She's taken," Sidney lied. "Sorry."

"Just my luck," he chuckled.

Nash reached over and grabbed Sidney's hand. "Hey."

Sidney turned to look at Nash. "What's up?"

"Peter was just telling me about how people are really getting into online trading."

"You mean stock trading?" Sidney leant forward to look past Nash to Peter. "I thought you worked for a brokerage firm?"

"I do, but I have clients who are constantly calling me for tips so they can delve into online trading. I was just telling Nash…"

"He'll teach me how to do it," Nash jumped in, cutting Peter off. "I'll have to pay a fee each time I trade, but if I really do my homework beforehand, I should be able to keep those to a minimum."

Sidney's eyebrows rose in surprise. He couldn't remember anything, outside of the bedroom, that had elicited such an excited reaction from Nash since they'd left Kansas. Nash had always pored over the stock section of the newspaper, something Sidney could never understand, especially because Nash had never had the money to invest in the market. "You'd do that?"

"Sure. Of course, as I told Nash, it would help if he'd take a few college classes. I doubt he'll ever become rich, but if he's good, he should make enough to live on."

"Is that the kind of thing you could teach over the phone?" Sidney asked.

"I like it here. I thought I'd stay another couple days."

"You can stay with us," Nash offered.

Sidney nodded his agreement. "Will it be expensive? The trading, I mean?"

"I can start showing him the ropes using my personal stocks." Peter reached in front of Nash and laid a hand on Sidney's arm. "Don't worry. We'll start slow. There are plenty of cheap stocks out there for Nash to cut his teeth on before threatening his savings."

Sidney glanced at Nash. He knew he'd give every cent in savings to keep that look of boyhood excitement on his lover's handsome face. "Does this mean you'll take some classes?"

"I know it sounds crazy," Nash mumbled, "but I'd really like to do this. I've always thought of stocks as the ultimate mind puzzle. You know, trying to figure out what would go up, what would go down? Now that I have a chance to learn, I'd really like to try it."

Sidney chuckled. "You don't need my permission to do this. You know that, right?" Sidney asked.

"It's not about permission," Nash said. "It's about your support."

Sidney leaned in and gave Nash a quick kiss. "My support is a given. You've done nothing but support me almost my entire life."

Nash kissed Sidney again before turning back to Peter. "Can we start this evening?"

Chapter Five

May 1992

After fumbling with the stack of newspapers in his hands, Sidney managed to get the front door shut. "Nash?"

"In here," Nash called from the kitchen.

Sidney set the papers on the coffee table and kicked off his shoes. He was flying on a high of praise he didn't know if he'd ever come down from. "Guess what?" he asked, stepping into the kitchen.

With his back to Sidney, Nash continued to stir the pot on the stove. "What?"

"I made the *Washington Post*'s article on '*Young Architects to Watch*'." He wrapped his arms around Nash's waist, needing to share the good news with the man who'd helped him get through college.

"I'm proud of you, babe," Nash said without turning around.

There was something in Nash's voice that sounded...off. Sidney stepped back. "Is there something wrong?"

"We don't have to talk about it now." Nash continued to stir his pot for several moments before finally turning around. "I really am proud of you." He leant forward and gave Sidney a quick kiss.

Sidney rested his hands on Nash's chest. "Please, talk to me."

Nash gestured towards the table. "I got my grades." He shook his head. "They're less than stellar."

Sidney walked to the table and lifted the sheet of paper. Nash was right, the grades weren't great, a C- and a D+. "You still passed them, though, right?"

"Barely," Nash mumbled.

Dropping the paper onto the table, Sidney rejoined Nash at the stove. He leaned against the counter because Nash had already turned back to preparing dinner. "I think you're too hard on yourself."

Nash looked at Sidney. "Really? How would you've reacted if you worked your ass off and got shitty grades?"

"Don't do that. You can't compare the two of us. I was a full-time student who didn't have to worry about getting up every day to work a job." Sidney pushed against Nash's shoulder until his partner turned to face him. He wished he could convince Nash to give up his job, but they'd had that argument before. "You do so much in a given day you make me dizzy. Work, online trading, school..." Sidney gestured to the bubbling spaghetti sauce. "And still find time to make sure I have a delicious meal at the end of the day. So you got a couple of lower than expected grades. So what? You're doing something you love."

"But I really tried," Nash said, staring over Sidney's shoulder. "I was stupid to think just because I had a passion for something I'd be good at it."

"That's bullshit. You *are* good at it. Unless you want an actual degree, every bit of knowledge you acquire will help you make money. You seem to have a natural gift for predicting trends in the market. Use that. I trust you with our money because I believe in your ability to make us more. I love you to the bottom of my heart, but I wouldn't just hand over money for you to play online games."

Nash eventually gazed down into Sidney's eyes. "I'll never be more than an online trader, will I?"

"That depends on what you really want. Every night I watch you either do homework or pore over the newspapers, looking for tips or trends, or whatever you call them. I know where your true passion lies. Do you?"

Nash nodded.

Sidney smiled up at his gorgeous partner. "Go with that feeling. If you can get the same knowledge by reading newspapers, do it. Having the ability to make a living at something you love is what's most important, not how you get there."

The sauce began to pop, painting the stove in drops of red. "I'd better finish dinner." Nash wrapped his arms around Sidney. "Thanks for the pep talk."

Sidney brushed a kiss across Nash's lips. "Never compare me to a cheerleader. I hated those bitches in school." He smiled again. "I just love you, and there are times when I think I believe in you more than you believe in yourself."

"You always have," Nash whispered.

* * * *

June 1992

Nash was in the middle of loading newspapers into the back of his truck to take to the recycling plant when he came across something that had the power to knock the wind out of him. He sat back on his ass and stared at the neatly bound bundle of *Washington Posts*. "Oh, no."

Bowing his head, he scrubbed the heel of his hands against his eyes. How had he forgotten? He vaguely remembered Sidney making the announcement of his achievement the previous month, but Nash had been so wrapped up in his stupid grades he'd let the moment pass without fanfare.

Sidney hadn't mentioned again that he'd been named a *'Young Architects to Watch'* in the newspaper, and, sadly, Nash hadn't remembered it. "Fuck!" he yelled to the empty house. He carried the stack of papers to the kitchen and set them on the table before picking up the phone. He ran his finger down the phone list tacked to the refrigerator before dialling.

"Hello?"

"Hi, Bobbi, it's Nash."

"Did something happen?" she asked, fear in her voice.

It was to be expected. Nash had never called Sidney's friend before, but, then again, he'd never had a reason to. "Sidney's fine. It's me who's fucked up." Nash went on to explain the situation he'd got himself into. By the time he'd finished, Bobbi had gone quiet. "Anyway, I was wondering if you could give me the name of a good restaurant in the city. Sidney's at the office trying to catch up on some work, so I thought I'd take the train in and surprise him with a nice dinner to make up for the fact that he has a self-centred asshole for a partner."

"He hasn't said anything about it, but I'd wondered why you weren't at the big celebration lunch the firm threw for him. When I asked him where you were, he just shook his head and gave me that *drop it* look. I assumed you couldn't get away or something."

Nash closed his eyes and rested his forehead against the fridge. "I didn't know anything about it."

"Don't be mad at him. It sounds to me like he didn't want to rub his career in your face."

"Yeah, it sounds like that to me, too. Hell, maybe a dinner won't be enough to smooth things over. Any ideas on what else I can do?" Nash knew he'd truly fucked things up. Selfish didn't begin to describe his actions.

"There are a lot of great places to eat in Chicago, but I can think of another place that he'd probably prefer."

"Where's that? I'll take him anywhere."

"Think hard, Nash. It's the one place he's always wanted you to take him."

"Wally's," Nash surmised.

"It's a thought anyway. I know he understands why you don't want him there, but I also know it hurts his feelings." Bobbi sighed. "I thought I was a good friend, but here I am spilling all the friend secrets I keep stashed away."

"Don't worry. I won't tell him. Thanks for your help."

"I'd do anything for him, you know that," Bobbi said.

"Yeah, I know. You're a good friend." Nash said goodbye before hanging up. He had some serious thinking to do before Sidney returned home.

* * * *

Just inside the front door, Sidney almost ran into a large framed *Washington Post* that was leaning against the hall table. He stared down at the highlighted article and melted.

"Do you like it?" Nash asked, coming into the room.

Sidney turned and launched himself into Nash's waiting arms. "I love it."

Nash walked them over to the sofa and pulled Sidney into his lap. "Strange thing happened to me earlier. I was cleaning out the storage room and ran across a stack of articles with the man I love highlighted in them." Nash brushed Sidney's cheek with his palm. "I'm sorry that I was so wrapped up in my own problems I didn't give you the recognition you deserve."

Sidney shrugged. "I knew you hadn't done it on purpose."

"Nope. No, I didn't, but I deserve a whack upside the head regardless." Nash ran his hand down Sidney's back to rest it on his ass. "I don't ever again want to put you in the position to downplay your successes. You deserve every accolade you receive, and from now on I want to be in the front row when your peers or the press recognise what I already know."

Sidney leaned against Nash's chest. "And what's that?" he asked, shamelessly fishing for one more compliment.

"That you're not only incredibly talented but hotter than hell," Nash said around a chuckle.

"I like that last bit the best," Sidney said. The last five minutes had almost made the entire episode worth it.

"Do you feel like going out to dinner with me? I found a special place that I think you'll love."

What Sidney really wanted was to stay in and snuggle, but it was obvious Nash needed him to go to this 'special place'. "Sure. Just let me run upstairs and put on a pair of jeans."

Before Sidney could get away, Nash pulled him in for a deep kiss. Sidney accepted Nash's tongue like he accepted everything else, with gusto. He moved to straddle Nash's lap, rubbing his erection against his man's hard torso.

Nash squeezed Sidney's ass before breaking the kiss. He reached down and ran a hand over Sidney's hard cock and chuckled. "Go get dressed," he said with a playful slap to Sidney's ass.

"Are you sure you wouldn't rather go to dinner tomorrow night?" Sidney offered.

Nash shook his head. "I won't be able to sleep tonight until I know I've done everything I could to make things up to you."

Sidney palmed Nash's cheek. "You're too hard on yourself, but then, you always have been." He brushed a kiss to Nash's nose. "What kind of partner would I be if I expected you to praise every little accomplishment?"

"What kind of partner would I be if I didn't want to praise your accomplishments?" Nash asked in return. "You *are* the single most important person in my life. Your success means more to me than my own."

A lump formed in Sidney's throat. He had no doubt Nash meant every word. The man had always been his champion, and, although Sidney tried to return all the love and support Nash gave him, he knew he sometimes came up lacking. "Two seconds," he said, jumping off Nash's lap.

He quickly changed into jeans and a T-shirt before rejoining Nash. "Five minutes," he noted. "I'm getting a lot better at this butch thing."

Laughing, Nash picked up his keys and ushered Sidney to the front door.

* * * *

Nash parked in front of Wally's and waited for Sidney's reaction.

With his lips pinched tight, Sidney shook his head. "You don't need to do this."

"Yes, I do. It's time I shared more of myself than I have been lately." Nash had put a good deal of thought into bringing Sidney to Wally's, and although he knew he was taking a chance it was the right thing to do. Hopefully his drinking buddies would welcome Sidney like they'd done him.

"Come on," he said, getting out of the truck.

Sidney sat in the pickup for several moments before eventually joining Nash on the sidewalk. "Will the guys you work with be here?"

Nash shrugged. "Not sure." He held the door open for Sidney before entering the bar. "Why don't you grab us a table while I get you a menu."

"Don't need one," Sidney said. "I want a cheddar burger and fries."

Nash stared at Sidney. "You know about those?"

"I had one that day I decorated for your birthday," Sidney mumbled.

Like a punch to the gut, Sidney's statement served to remind Nash of another of his colossal fuck-ups and the wrapper he'd later found in the trash. He gestured towards an empty table, discreetly waving to people he knew. As he settled in his chair, he leaned his forearms on the table. "Would you like me to introduce you around?"

"No, that's okay. It's enough that you brought me in the first place."

"I should've done it a long time ago."

One of Nash's favourite waitresses came over to the table and rested her hand on Nash's shoulder. "Hey, honey."

"Hi, Vickie." Nash smiled up at the attractive woman before gesturing to Sidney. "I'd like you to meet my…"

"Sidney," Sidney introduced himself, cutting Nash off.

"Nice to meet you." Vickie thumped Nash on the shoulder. "What can I get you two this evening?"

"Two cheddar burgers, one well, one medium well, fries and two Coors Lights," Nash ordered.

"Coming right up."

As soon as Vickie was gone, Nash eyed Sidney. "I was going to introduce you as my partner."

"I know. That's why I stopped you." Sidney started to reach across the table but quickly pulled his hand back. "I don't want to do anything to ruin this place for you."

"You won't," Nash stated in a matter-of-fact tone.

"There's a guy at the bar that keeps smiling at us," Sidney whispered.

Nash glanced over his shoulder. He couldn't help but laugh at the goofy look on Butch's face. "That's my buddy, Butch."

Sidney's eyebrows shot up. "That's Butch?"

"Yeah. Let me introduce you." He narrowed his eyes at Sidney. "As my partner." Nash raised his hand and waved at his friend. "Wipe that look off your ugly mug and get over here."

"Ugly is definitely not how I would describe him," Sidney mumbled.

"Don't let on that you think he's handsome or he'll be stuck like glue to you all night. Believe me, I've seen it happen with almost every single woman who walks in this place."

Sidney rested his elbow on the table and cupped his cheek, subtly trying to hide his scarred face. Nash wanted to say something, but Butch crossed the room before he could.

"I told Vickie I'd bring these over. What're you doing here on a Saturday night?" Butch asked, setting three mugs of beer on the table.

Nash reached for his beer. "I thought it was about damn time I brought Sidney over for a burger." He gestured to Sidney. "This is the pain-in-the-ass I work with every day. Butch, this is my partner, Sidney."

Butch was the first to reach across the table and offer his hand. It took Sidney several moments to uncover his palmed cheek and accept the handshake. "Nice to meet you," Butch said.

"You, too," Sidney replied. "Despite what he just said, Nash speaks highly of you."

Butch glanced at Nash. "I could say the same to you."

Nash knew Butch was lying to save Sidney's feelings. Although Nash had told his friend bits and pieces of his life with Sidney, he hadn't gone into any details about their relationship.

When Butch's gaze went back to Sidney's scar, Nash knew he'd done both men a disservice by not telling Butch about Sidney's accident.

"I can see why Nash hasn't brought you here before," Butch commented.

Nash exploded out of his chair and towered over Butch, ready to put the asshole in his place. His friend looked up at him and grinned. "What? You the jealous type? I wasn't planning to make a play for him, just admiring. Relax, dude."

Nash sat back down, wind let out of his sails. Shame on him for assuming Butch was referring to Sidney's scarred face. *Wait a minute.* Nash rubbed his eyes. "Are you telling me you're attracted to him?" he asked.

Butch looked at Nash like he was stupid. "What's not to be attracted to?"

"Hello? Sitting right here," Sidney reminded them. Although Sidney acted annoyed by the brief exchange, Nash could tell his man was secretly pleased with the idea that Butch liked him.

"Sorry," Nash said to Sidney before turning his attention back to Butch. "Didn't know you were gay."

"Don't worry. You're not my type," Butch said around a laugh. He stared at Sidney again. "But you? Oh, yeah."

For some reason the comment bristled. "What's wrong with me?" Nash asked.

"Too big. Too pig-headed. Take your pick," Butch answered, lifting his beer to his lips.

Vickie approached the table with Nash and Sidney's burgers. "Here you go, honey."

"Thanks." Nash moved the small cup of spicy ranch dressing closer to his plate.

"Ooh, what's that?" Sidney asked.

Nash dipped a fry into the dressing and passed it to Sidney. "Try it. I've tried to get 'em to tell me how they make it but so far nada."

"Mmm." Sidney smiled up at Vickie. "Can I get some of that?"

"You betcha."

Nash bit into his burger and moaned. Wally's mixed a generous amount of shredded sharp cheddar cheese inside the burger instead of just laying a slab of cheese on top. The result was incredible. Lost in his love for the cheddar burger, Nash was brought back to earth by Sidney.

"Just as good as I remembered," Sidney mumbled with his mouth full of food.

"Shit. Joe's here," Butch announced. "I'll go head him off. Challenge him to a game of pool or something." Beer in hand, he stood and smiled at Sidney once again before shaking his head. "Damn."

Nash watched his buddy cross the room towards one of their co-workers. "I honestly had no idea he was gay."

"Probably bi." Sidney dunked a fry into the dressing Vickie had set next to him at some point during their conversation. "I wouldn't take it personally."

Nash couldn't put his finger on why the news bothered him as much as it did. Maybe because he'd thought he was alone in his sexual preferences at work. He'd always had to laugh along with the jokes his co-workers made, even if they were against gays. Nash wasn't sure if it helped or hurt to know Butch had been playing the same game.

* * * *

Bright and early Monday morning, Nash cornered Butch in the break room. "Why didn't you tell me?"

"Tell you what?" Butch asked, feeding quarters into the junk food machine.

"You know damn well what." Nash leaned his shoulder against the machine.

"What exactly did you want me to tell you? That I've enjoyed sticking my cock in a dude's ass before?" Butch's voice went lower. "Because it's no one's business." Butch bent over and retrieved his bag of chips. "I shouldn't have said that about your boyfriend, and I'm sorry for that, but that doesn't mean I want to talk about my sex life with you or anyone else."

Nash held up his hands. "Whoa. I didn't mean to piss ya off. Just thought we were friends." Nash pushed off from the machine and started to walk out of the room.

"Wait," Butch called him back.

Nash stopped walking but didn't turn around.

"You're the only real friend I've got. The gay thing just isn't something I'm comfortable talking about."

Nash nodded. "Good enough. I won't bring it up again." He left the room before he could say more. It wasn't like he'd expected Butch to huddle with him in the corner and talk about butt sex all day, for crying out loud. It simply would've been nice to know he had someone to talk to if he'd needed to.

Nash went back to the car he'd been working on earlier and tried to get his mind back on the job at hand.

"We cool?" Butch asked from behind him.

"Yeah, we're cool."

"Grab a beer with me after work?"

"Sure," Nash answered. Whatever Butch's problem was with being gay, it had nothing to do with Nash and he needed to remember that.

Chapter Six

June 1993

The Metra slowed to a stop, and the man sitting across from Sidney disembarked the commuter train. *Thank God.* Tired to the bone, Sidney rested his feet on the vacant seat and continued to stare out of the window.

Not only had he spent the previous four months working on a generic-looking design for an office high-rise, but the customers had requested changes to make the building appear even more boring. What the hell? Did corporations not understand that a fun and unique design was a morale booster to the thousands of drones who were forced to enter it each day?

Unfortunately, Miles, McShane and Frawling, Inc, the architectural firm he worked for, were all about pleasing the customers instead of trying to convince them to think outside the box. When the big guns for Drelling Electronics had asked that all rounded corners on the outside of the buildings be squared off, in an effort to save costs, the firm had immediately agreed and had ordered Sidney to make the changes in design.

If it hadn't been for Bobbi, Sidney had no doubt he'd have told them to fuck off and walked out. His quirky colleague had immediately picked up on Sidney's frustration and had spirited him away from the office for a long lunch. They'd eaten dessert for their meal, and Bobbi had allowed him the opportunity to vent his frustrations.

Now, as he rode the train towards home, the disappointments with his chosen career began to creep back to the forefront of his mind. It had always been his dream to create unique buildings. Although he'd told himself a thousand times that every architect had to pay their dues with small, boring structures while they learned the ins and outs of the business, it was pure torture for him.

The Metra slowed to a stop, and Sidney gathered his leather messenger bag along with the tube of blueprints he'd promised to go over and make changes to and got in line to get off the train. If he was lucky, he'd have time for a quick dinner with Nash before he had to clear the table and get down to work. He hated not spending time with Nash after a long day, but his partner would no doubt be on the computer anyway.

With Peter's guidance, Nash had begun to make a nice portfolio for them. Although he still continued to work at the garage, Nash would soon be in the position to trade online full-time. *Odd.* Now that Nash was finally happy, it was Sidney who seemed to be in a constant state of discontentment.

As he drove the short distance home from the station, Sidney wondered what life would've been like had they stayed at the ranch. It had been three years since they'd moved to Chicago and they'd yet to go back to Kansas for a visit. At first he hadn't mentioned the ranch out of respect for Nash. The transition to Lake Forest hadn't been easy for his handsome cowboy, and the last thing Sidney had wanted was to rub salt in an exposed wound.

Now that Nash seemed more content with his life, Sidney wondered if it wasn't the time to go back for a short visit. Nash still spoke with Tommy every month or so over the phone, keeping himself updated on the success of the Running E, but he hadn't mentioned going back. Maybe a week away would do them both some good. Lord knew, Sidney was ready to get the hell away from work for a few days.

Arriving home, he was happy to see Nash's pickup. Nothing would feel better at that moment than being in the strong arms of the man he loved. He quickly gathered his things and raced to the door.

Entering the town house, he was disappointed by the empty living room. "Nash?"

"Up here," Nash called from the second floor.

With an eye towards the staircase, Sidney groaned and dropped his bag and blueprints on the couch before heading up. He didn't smell anything cooking, which meant Nash had his nose pressed against the computer screen.

Just as he'd suspected, Nash was at his small desk in the spare bedroom. Evidently he'd been so anxious to monitor his investments he hadn't bothered to take a shower or even change out of his greasy work clothes.

One look at Nash's filthy T-shirt and Sidney cringed at the thought of his tailored dress shirt getting ruined. He immediately began unbuttoning and by the time he had crossed the small room, he was wearing only his lightweight undershirt.

Sidney draped his arms over Nash's shoulders and kissed his cheek. "It feels so good to be home."

After several keystrokes, Nash turned away from the screen and looked up at Sidney. "Bad day?"

Sidney nodded. He needed the love and comfort only Nash could provide. Despite his rumbling stomach and the work to be done on the blueprints, he quickly rid himself of his shoes and dress pants before straddling Nash's lap.

Nash wrapped his arms around Sidney, pulling him closer. "What's going on?"

"Same old thing. I know you're busy, but I just need to feel you for a moment." Sidney buried his face against Nash's neck. His partner smelled of hard work. Sidney suddenly felt guilty. Nash sweated his ass off all day only to come home and spend his evenings working online, and there he was whining about his air-conditioned, non-physical job. He bit his bottom lip. "Sorry."

Nash lifted the back of Sidney's undershirt and ran his hands across his skin. "For what? Needing me? Never apologise for that."

"No, for belly aching like a five-year-old." Despite the salty taste, Sidney couldn't resist kissing and licking the bronzed skin of Nash's neck. He worked his way to Nash's mouth, putting them nose to nose. "I love you," he whispered against Nash's lips.

With one hand working its way under the waistband of Sidney's briefs, Nash closed the distance and kissed him.

Sidney opened his mouth on Nash's exploring tongue and groaned. Yes, this is what he needed. It didn't matter that Nash couldn't do a damn thing about Sidney's bullshit problems at work. The fact that he supported him once he returned home was enough. It was the overwhelming love he received from Nash that made the rest of the world take a backseat, even if only for a few hours.

Nash pulled out of the kiss and stared at Sidney. "Why don't you call and order pizza while I take a shower? I got a new video in the mail today. We can spend the rest of the night in bed, eating pizza and gettin' off."

"Is it the kind of video that comes in a brown wrapper?" Sidney asked. Nash had amassed quite a collection of porn since the early days of their relationship.

The grin on Nash's face was the only answer Sidney needed. He hated to tell his partner he had work to do. Sidney thought of the blueprints waiting for him downstairs. After a quick determination of what was most important in his life, he nodded. "You've got yourself a deal."

* * * *

Nash took another bite of the pepperoni pizza Sidney held up to him. "You're spoiling me," he said after swallowing.

Sidney brushed the slice of pizza across Nash's nipple. "I have loads of spoiling to do before I can even hope to catch up with you." He licked the grease from Nash's chest before sucking the sensitive nipple into his mouth.

Nash took the pizza from Sidney's hand and tossed it towards the box. Although he and Sidney still enjoyed a healthy sex life, a quickie in the kitchen or before dropping off to sleep at night didn't compare to the lovemaking they'd already enjoyed that evening.

Sidney released the nipple and began licking his way down Nash's chest. "I can taste my cum on your skin," he said, glancing up at Nash.

"I don't doubt it." Nash threaded his fingers through Sidney's shoulder-length hair. God, he loved the way the silky black strands felt against his callused hands. It had taken Sidney a while, but he'd eventually agreed to let his hair grow again. Nash had tried not to pressure him into it, but he was thankful when Sidney had finally decided on his own.

Before Sidney could shimmy further down the bed, Nash gave a subtle tug to his hair. "Swing that sweet ass around here," Nash told him.

Sidney shook his head. "I'd rather suck you while you watch that movie again."

Nash chuckled. "Yeah, it did get me pretty damn worked up."

"I'll say." Sidney grinned. "But I liked it."

"Okay, babe, I'm all yours," Nash said, satisfied that Sidney was taken care of. He reached for the VCR remote and hit play. A darkened bar filled the screen with dozens of men sitting at various tables. The men began to pair up and within five minutes cocks were proudly on display.

Nash hadn't told Sidney earlier, but the bar in the movie reminded him a lot of Wally's. Not that Wally's was the spot to go for gay orgies, but the layout was incredibly similar. When a smaller man walked into the scene and was quickly surrounded by two big men, Nash couldn't help but moan.

Never before had he fantasised about sharing Sidney with another man, but there was something about the third man in the movie that reminded him of Butch.

As he watched the two men slowly strip the new arrival, Nash continued to run his hands through Sidney's hair, imagining it was Butch at his side, readying Sidney to be fucked.

With a loud groan, Nash reached for the lube. He dislodged Sidney's mouth from his cock and slicked the steel hard shaft. "Need you," he grunted, holding his cock by its base.

Sidney moved to straddle Nash's hips. "Like this?"

"No." Placing his hands under Sidney's arms, Nash tossed him to the mattress before rolling to come down on top of him. It only took a second to assure himself that Sidney's body was still stretched from their previous lovemaking.

Nash found his partner's waiting hole with the crown of his cock and slowly entered its heated depth. "Fuck," he growled, closing his eyes. The threesome on the screen had not only excited him, it had also served to send a deep level of disturbance through his heart. How could he even think of sharing Sidney with someone else? Sidney was the only man he'd ever needed, the only one he'd ever wanted for more than a quick fuck.

As Nash pistoned in and out of Sidney's body, he held nothing back. He couldn't explain it, even to himself, but the lust coursing through his veins at the idea of a threesome quickly gave way to anger. Unfortunately, Sidney was currently paying for the internal war raging within Nash.

Opening his eyes, he stared down at the gorgeous creature under him. Head back, neck exposed, Sidney appeared to be completely oblivious to Nash's thoughts. How could he have forgotten how much his lover enjoyed a punishing fuck? Had the two of them become so settled in their lives together that important details of their sex life had begun to take a backseat?

Nash sank his teeth into Sidney's neck, delivering a bite that wouldn't soon fade. Sidney cried out, shooting warmth between them, but Nash wasn't finished. He lifted Sidney's legs to drape over his shoulders as he continued the relentless rhythm. "You're mine," he grunted over and over.

Sidney's eyes opened. "Never doubt it."

Nash drove deep, with one final slam of his hips, as the first strand of seed burst from his cock. He collapsed on top of Sidney, trying to shut out the three distinct voices on the television. *Never going to happen*, he told himself as he struggled to regain his composure. He wrapped his arms around Sidney and rolled over, putting the thinner man on top of him.

"Is that what you want?" Sidney asked out of nowhere.

"What?" Nash asked, looking up at Sidney.

Sidney glanced over his shoulder at the movie. "A threesome?"

Nash opened his mouth to deny the assumption but couldn't get the words out. "Just a momentary fantasy," he finally admitted. "Doesn't mean I want to do it. Hell, I've never even thought about it before this movie."

Sidney rested his head against Nash's shoulder and kissed his neck. "I've never made love to two men at the same time."

"And hopefully you never will."

Sidney rose up. "What? You can fantasise but I can't?"

"Didn't say that. You can think about fucking someone other than me, but actually doing it is a whole different matter."

Sidney's eyes narrowed as he seemed to consider Nash's words. "That goes for you, too, right?"

"Of course. People are tempted to stray all the time, but it's their choice whether or not to act on it. Cheating isn't something I believe in."

"Even if Brad Pitt came walking through the door, cock in hand?"

Nash scratched his chin, pretending to consider the possibility of the mouth-watering star of *A River Runs Through It* dropping in for a quick fuck. "Only if you'd join us, and only with Brad Pitt."

Sidney held up his pinkie finger. "I swear."

Nash hooked his pinkie with Sidney before settling Sidney's head back against him. "You're the only man for me."

With a snort, Sidney bit Nash's chin. "Unless a blond-haired, blue-eyed stud breaks down the door."

"That's not true," Nash reprimanded. "I'd let him in without making him break the door." He stopped Sidney's hand before the playful slap could land and laughed. "We need more evenings like this together."

"Yeah," Sidney sighed. "Would you mind turning the movie off?"

Nash grabbed the remote and switched off the television. "You ready to tell me what's bothering you?"

"It's nothing, really, just work," Sidney said around a yawn. "There are days I think that damn place is sucking the creativity out of me."

"So what's the alternative?" Nash asked.

"To find another job and design even more boring buildings for stuffy corporations," Sidney mumbled.

"Have you thought of starting your own design company?" Nash asked.

"Yeah, but I need a couple more years of hands-on experience before I'm qualified to tackle something like that." Sidney kissed Nash's chin. "Besides, I'm waiting for my partner to make me rich. How're our stocks doing?"

"Peter said we should hang on to the Apple stocks even though they're pretty stagnant, but he told me to buy Coca-Cola. That's what I was trying to figure out when you came in and distracted me."

"I love Coke."

Nash hugged Sidney. *God I love this man.* "I do, too, babe, but I'm not sure I can do it and still keep the other stocks. Something's got to give, and I can't decide which one to dump." Although he rarely talked with Sidney about the pressures he felt gambling with their savings, some decisions needed to be made by both of them.

Sidney reached behind his back and directed Nash's hand towards his ass. Nash got the hint and ran his fingers over Sidney's leaking hole before pushing three inside. After years spent together, Nash knew it was more for comfort on Sidney's part than a sexual need.

"I believe in you," Sidney whispered. "Take more money out of our savings. We haven't touched any of the ranch money Tommy sends. Use that."

"That's your money," Nash started to argue.

"No. That's our money. The Running E's just as much yours as it is mine."

"But what if Peter's wrong and we lose it?" Although not a fortune, the ranch account held a sizeable amount of money.

"We can't lose the ranch. It's been paid off for years. But, if it makes you feel better, leave enough in the account to cover taxes for the next few years until our investments start paying off."

"You should use that money to start your own company." Nash didn't want the added pressure of gambling everything they had.

"Someday," Sidney replied. "But it'll take a lot more money than is in the ranch account. The only way I'll be able to afford to strike out on my own is if we start drinking lots and lots of Coke."

* * * *

November 1993

Nash set down his beer and stared across the table at Butch. Although he'd known the man for a few years, he knew absolutely nothing about his family or where he'd come from. Whenever he asked anything personal, Butch either changed the subject or got annoyed, so Nash had learned quickly to stay clear of the topic. "What're you doing for Thanksgiving?"

Butch signalled for another beer. "Same thing I do every year."

Nash sighed. "And what's that?"

"Why're you being so damn nosy today?" Butch asked. "Thanks, honey," he said, taking the mug of cold beer from Vickie.

Nash knew he should probably drop it, but he was sick and tired of the walls Butch kept in place. "Because outside of Sidney, you're the best damn friend I've ever had, but I know fuck-all about you."

"Nothing to know. I grew up in this nation's joke of a foster care system. Graduated high school by the skin of my teeth, did a short stint in the Navy and moved here. Been working at the garage ever since." Butch shrugged. "That's my life in a nutshell."

There was obviously more to Butch's story, but it was a start. "So…Thanksgiving?" Nash prompted, hoping to finally get an answer.

"You can't celebrate what you don't have. For me, it's just a day off work."

"Celebrate it with us. Sidney and I usually go to Philadelphia to spend time with the Ballentines, but Maggie and Alan are in Tampa helping Maggie's brother through the final stages of pancreatic cancer. We've invited the rest of the clan to Chicago, but I doubt they'll come."

Butch shook his head. "I'm not good with people I don't know."

"That's bullshit. You charm everyone who walks into this place," Nash argued.

"I'm not good with families! Okay!" Butch shouted, drawing the attention of the people seated around them.

Normally, Nash would back down, but there was something so raw about Butch's display of emotions that he couldn't let it drop. He leaned on the table, putting his face directly in front of Butch. "Three, maybe four people, sitting around a table stuffing their faces with turkey. I'm asking you to come. Please, do this for me if not for yourself."

Butch took another drink of his beer. "We'll see."

* * * *

"Fuck!" Butch howled when he set the sleeper sofa down on his foot. "I can't believe you bought a new couch when the old one was perfectly good."

"It wasn't a sleeper," Nash replied. Truth be told, he didn't like the new couch as much as the old one. Comfort was a high priority in his book when it came to furniture, and no matter how expensive a sleeper sofa was it couldn't compare to the softness of a regular couch.

"Perfect," Sidney said, coming into the room. He pulled his coat out of the closet and grabbed his keys. "I'm on my way to the airport. Just remember to roll up the rug before we get back," he instructed, kissing Nash on the lips.

"I'll remember." Nash gave Sidney a swat on the ass. His partner had been flitting around the house for two days, trying to make sure everything was as accommodating to Luke as they could make it. "Honk when you pull up outside and Butch and I'll be out."

By the time Sidney left the town house, Butch had already retrieved a beer from the refrigerator. He sat in Nash's recliner, instead of on the new sofa, and took a drink. "So what's the deal with this guy who's coming in? Is he really worth buying a new couch for?"

"Yeah, he is." Nash was the first of them to sit on the sofa. "Luke's an old friend of Sidney's. I told you he was paralysed from the waist down in a car wreck, but I didn't tell you Sidney was behind the wheel when they struck the deer. Although Sidney denies it, I know he still carries a lot of guilt over it."

Butch whistled. "That's rough."

Nash put his feet up on the coffee table, hoping to get comfortable. "It gets worse. Luke was in a relationship with his physical therapist for a couple of years when he found out the guy had a fiancée on the side. Brian was an okay guy. He just wasn't willing to come out to his family."

"Fucker," Butch mumbled under his breath. "So there'll be yet another marriage based on lies." He shook his head. "I may not be out and proud, but I'd never expect someone else to suffer because of it."

Butch's statement opened a door Nash couldn't pass up. "Why aren't you out? I mean, I understand the work thing, but is that all there is to it?"

"Drop it," Butch grumbled. "I'm here, aren't I? Just be happy with that."

Once again, Nash was left with more questions. He couldn't help but wonder if Butch would ever be completely honest with him.

* * * *

It took several moments of manoeuvring to get Luke into the car, and by the time Sidney climbed behind the wheel his hands were beet red and numb. Luke really needed to invest in a lighter chair.

"Damn, it's cold out there," Luke commented.

"That's Chicago for ya." Sidney started the car before pulling out of the parking lot. He glanced over at Luke's handsome profile. His friend looked pale, too pale. "Was the flight okay?"

"Yeah, except for this thing." Luke tapped the urinary drainage bag strapped to his leg. Although the bag was barely noticeable under the loose-legged pants, Sidney couldn't imagine how uncomfortable it must be.

"Don't worry. We've got a ground floor bathroom at the town house," Sidney assured his friend.

Luke watched the scenery out of the side window for several moments before speaking again. "Feels weird being here without Brian," he mumbled.

Sidney took one hand off the wheel and reached across the console. He threaded his fingers through Luke's and gently squeezed. "I'm sorry."

Luke shrugged. "It doesn't hurt as much anymore. I've moved on to pissed."

Sidney chuckled. "As well you should be."

"I thought he didn't want anyone to know because he was afraid for his job. Hell, I didn't even know he had family in town. Brian said he moved to Philly from San Diego. I just assumed his family was still there when he agreed to Thanksgivings at my folks' house."

There wasn't much Sidney could say. Brian had fooled all of them, not just Luke. He decided to change the subject. "How's Josh?"

"Good, I guess. Mom says he's still clean if that's what you're asking, although I seriously doubt it. He'll graduate in May with his Bachelor's. Not sure if he'll go on for his Master's though."

"Things still strained between the two of you?" Sidney asked.

"Some. Maybe he's just busy with school, but he rarely comes around and almost never returns my calls, unless, of course, he needs money. Mom said to give him time to find his way again."

"But?" Sidney sensed there was something more.

"But how much time should I waste on someone like him? It's time he fucking grew up and stopped making everything about him. It was the same way in high school, but I thought he'd finally gotten over himself."

It was as if Luke was talking about someone Sidney had never met. "What was he like in high school?"

"A stoner. Mom and Dad don't know, so don't you dare say anything to them, but he used to get high pretty regularly, even back then. He refused to come to any of my games, making one excuse after another, but he always came home at night smelling of weed."

Sidney thought back to their early friendship. "He smoked a joint a couple times a week at school, but I wouldn't have called him a stoner."

"Whatever," Luke said, continuing to stare out the side window. "I'm tired of reaching out to him. Hell, I've got my own problems to deal with."

"You mean the Brian thing?"

"What?" Luke turned his head to look at Sidney. "You should know me better than that. What Brian did was shitty, but it wasn't enough to ruin my life. No, I think I'm ready for a change."

"What kind of change?" Sidney asked.

Luke tapped the dashboard with his fingers. "Promise you won't think less of me if I tell you?"

Sidney reached across and put a hand on Luke's shoulder. "Oh, Luke, you know there's no way I could think less of you than I already do," Sidney joked.

Luke rolled his eyes but cracked a slight smile. "God, I've missed you."

"I've missed you, too, now tell me your super secret."

Luke continued to tap on the dashboard nervously. "I've really enjoyed myself since Mom and Dad went to Florida. I love them to pieces, but they both tend to hover. It doesn't seem to matter that I haven't lived at home with them for a while. They find some excuse to stop by almost on a daily basis."

"They worry," Sidney reminded Luke.

"I know that, but they don't need to. I'm capable of taking care of myself, and if I *do* need something, I'm also quite capable of using the phone."

Sidney nodded his understanding. "So what're you thinking?"

Luke grinned. "I'm a graphic designer. I can work from anywhere." He made a point of gesturing out of the windshield. "Although it's colder than fuck outside, Chicago's looking pretty good."

Sidney was floored by Luke's answer. "Seriously?"

"What? You don't want me?" Luke chuckled.

"Just the opposite. I'd love to have you close." Sidney wondered whether or not he should say anything about the job in Saudi Arabia his boss had been working on acquiring. He hadn't mentioned it to Nash because there was no way in hell he'd move Nash to a country where they weren't allowed to openly love each other. Unfortunately, his boss had said without words that his career with the firm depended on him taking the project if they were lucky enough to get it.

"Good, because I've already called a realtor. I've got an appointment to look at apartments on Friday."

Sidney couldn't believe how fast Luke was moving. "Have you even talked to Maggie and Alan about it?"

Luke shook his head. "They'll try to talk me out of it."

"Of course they will," Sidney agreed. The Ballentine boys were all grown and out of the house. He hated to tell Luke that Alan and Maggie probably felt he was the only one left who needed looking after. Luke didn't, of course, but that was beside the point.

"I need a change, Sid. I know they won't understand, but I really need this."

Sidney took a deep breath. "Okay. Then I'll do everything I can to help."

They continued to discuss different areas of the city until Sidney pulled up in front of the house. "Well, this is home," he announced.

Luke looked from the town house to Sidney. "Stairs."

"Yeah, but I've got that covered." He honked the horn and pointed towards the front door. Moments later Nash and Butch stepped out on to the landing.

"Who's that?" Luke asked.

"Nash's best friend Butch." Sidney had to admit Butch looked like a badass, but he'd turned out to be a very nice man.

"Butch? What kind of name is that?"

Sidney gestured towards the bald man striding towards them. "It fits. Just look at him."

The passenger door was pulled open before Luke could comment. "How do we want to do this?" Butch asked.

Luke glanced at Sidney with fear in his eyes. Sidney took the keys out of the ignition and climbed out of the car. "Hang tight." He opened the trunk and waited for Nash to retrieve Luke's wheelchair and suitcase. "We'll just need help getting him and the chair up the steps," Sidney informed Butch.

"Why don't I just carry him up to the house and Nash can get the chair?" Butch asked.

"No!" Luke was quick to shout. He seemed to realise how his outburst could be taken and calmed his voice. "I mean, I think it would be better to ease the chair up with me in it."

"Nonsense," Butch said, scooping Luke out of the car seat and into his arms. "Wrap your arms around my neck, and I'll have you inside in two seconds."

Sidney turned his head to hide his smile at the utter shock written all over Luke's face as Butch carried him swiftly up the steps. "Luke's gonna make me pay for that," he mumbled to Nash.

"Better you than me," Nash whispered back, hoisting the wheelchair off the ground.

Chapter Seven

November 1993

After stowing Luke's suitcase in the coat closet, Nash joined Sidney in the kitchen. "What're you doing?" he asked, wrapping his arms around his partner.

Sidney hung up the phone and leant back against Nash. "Maggie made me promise I'd call when Luke made it in." He looked up at Nash. "Don't you dare tell him."

Butch came barrelling into the kitchen. "The little fella wants a beer. Is that okay?"

Nash laughed. "He's six-two. In what world is that considered little?"

"Six-two? Really?" Butch's eyebrows drew together. "He seems so much smaller."

"That's because compared to you he is. Whatever you do, don't treat him any different than you do anyone else," Sidney warned.

Butch paused in the act of pulling two beers out of the fridge. "That's stupid. He is different. Are you telling me I should've told him to get his own damn drink?"

"No, that's not what I'm saying. Just don't baby him because he can't walk. He's a proud man who's been living on his own for a while." Sidney glanced up at Nash. "He told me on the way over that he's thinking of moving here to get away from Maggie and Alan's constant hovering." Sidney shook his finger at Nash before turning the waving wand on Butch. "So, no hovering. Got it?"

Nash wasn't immediately pleased by the unexpected news. "Got it," he absently agreed. Luke was a great guy, and Nash had always enjoyed his company, but he also knew Luke's presence often took a toll on Sidney. Despite Sidney's protests to the contrary, Nash knew Sidney still felt guilty at times.

Butch disappeared without a word, leaving Nash alone to address Luke's decision with Sidney. "Why here?"

"I think he likes the idea of moving to a bigger city."

"So why not New York?" Nash asked.

"Because it isn't far enough away." Sidney turned around and looked up at Nash. "I know he feels crowded by his parents, but I think it also has something to do with Josh."

The expression on Sidney's face told Nash there was more to the story. "What about Josh?"

Sidney sighed. "Luke thinks he's using again."

Nash had had just about all he could stand of Josh Ballentine. "I won't have him in my house if he's using."

"I know," Sidney mumbled. "I reckon he does too, which is why he didn't come for Thanksgiving."

Sidney reached up and ran his hands through Nash's hair. "Luke's dead set on moving away from his family. I'd just feel a lot better if he was close enough to ask for help if he needed it."

Staring down into Sidney's light green eyes, Nash couldn't do anything but nod his agreement. For someone who'd been raised by an asshole like Jackson Wilks, Sidney sure as hell had a big heart. "Do you think we have time to sneak upstairs for a quickie?"

Sidney chuckled. "No, but I'm sure Luke's tired after his trip, so I doubt he'll want to stay up late. Does that help?"

Nash rubbed his hardening cock against Sidney. "Not really, but I'll take what I can get."

"Oh, you'll get it, just not for a few hours."

* * * *

After stuffing themselves with turkey, dressing and cranberry sauce, the four of them collapsed in the living room. Nash was sound asleep on the floor with his head propped up on one of the new sofa cushions, Sidney made himself comfortable in the recliner while Butch and Luke pored over the real estate section of the paper.

Sidney couldn't get over how well Butch and Luke got along, or how Butch seemed to hang on Luke's every word. As Sidney fought to keep his eyes open, he listened to the two men.

"No, not that one," Butch said.

"Why? It looks big," Luke replied.

"Yep, but it's not in a good neighbourhood. It'd be better to take a smaller place in a better part of town. Hopefully somewhere with a doorman."

Sidney smiled to himself. For all Butch's bluster, it was nice to see the softer side of the Mr Clean look-alike. It was also nice to know he wouldn't be the only one in town looking out for Luke should he move to Chicago.

* * * *

December 1993

The ringing phone woke Sidney out of a sound sleep. He sat up straight and lunged for the phone. There was only one reason someone called in the middle of the night and Sidney's gut clenched. "Hello?"

"Who the fuck do you think you are?"

"Josh?" Sidney rubbed the sleep from his eyes and leaned against the headboard. "What's wrong?"

"Mom told me what you did. She and Dad are beside themselves at the prospect of Luke moving. What the hell did you say to convince him to move, or did something happen between the three of you when he stayed there last month?"

Sidney moved off the bed in an effort to keep Nash from taking the phone from him. "Are you high?" he asked.

"This isn't about me, so butt your nose out of my business. I wanna know if you're fucking my brother!"

Sidney took a calming breath. He felt like handing the phone to Nash and walking away from the conversation. How long could he continue to hold on to a friendship that hadn't been there in years? "I'm hanging up the phone. Don't call me again unless you're sober enough to talk sensibly."

Hanging up the handset took every ounce of strength Sidney possessed. "I think he's using again," he mumbled, tears filling his eyes.

"That sonofabitch!" Nash exploded. "What did he say to you?"

Sidney wiped his eyes before the tears had a chance to fall. "Nothing important. He's upset that Luke's moving to Chicago."

Nash pulled Sidney on to the bed and into his arms. "Don't lie to me. I can tell there was more to the conversation."

"He accused me...us of fucking Luke while he was here for Thanksgiving." Before the words had finished leaving his mouth the phone rang again.

Nash reached for the phone, easily holding Sidney back when he attempted to intervene in what he knew would be a friendship-ending conversation. Nash snatched up the handset. "Listen up, you fucking asshole. Don't you ever call this house again. Sidney's been nothing but kind and patient with you, but I've had enough of you throwing it back in his face."

Nash slammed down the phone before reaching out and pulling the cord from the wall. He turned towards Sidney with rage in his eyes. Nash opened his mouth but quickly snapped it shut.

"Nash?" Sidney prayed Nash wasn't angry with him over something Josh had said.

Nash's handsome face softened. "I'm sorry, babe, but I think it's time you washed your hands of him."

Closing his eyes, Sidney shook his head. He tried to picture his life without Josh. Nash was right, Josh hadn't been much of a friend in a long while, but there had been a time when things had been different. It was those times that he couldn't bring himself to let go of.

He opened his eyes and swallowed around the lump in his throat. "I keep asking myself how I could walk away from my own father without a second thought, but I can't bring myself to do the same to Josh."

"And did you come up with an answer?"

"Yeah." Sidney coughed to clear his throat. "Josh's problem is drugs. He's fucked up, but he still has the one thing I don't think my father ever possessed."

"What's that?" Nash asked.

"A soul worth saving."

* * * *

February 1994

Box in hand, Sidney stared at his work station. He'd worked his ass off for three and a half years only to be given an ultimatum on the new Saudi Arabian dream complex. If the job had been in a gay-friendly nation, Sidney would've jumped at the chance to design a building with no expense spared.

"So you're really leaving?" Bobbi asked.

Sidney set the box on his chair. "Looks that way."

"You could probably sue them, you know."

"No, I can't. *Officially* I quit. It was a choice they gave me over termination." It would be unlikely he'd be able to file for unemployment benefits, but at least he wouldn't have a termination on his employment record.

"Feel like getting a drink?" Bobbi asked.

"Can't. I've gotta figure out a way to tell Nash, and, believe me, alcohol won't help."

"Does he know about the offer?"

"No, which makes it even worse. I should've told him months ago when the job first came up. I was stupid to think they'd let me design the building without overseeing its construction."

Bobbi stepped forward and gave Sidney a hug. "It's not fair. You're the best architect here."

"Thanks, but sometimes being the best isn't enough." He hated to admit it, but he'd known since the beginning that the partners at Miles, McShane and Frawling weren't at all comfortable with his sexuality. He'd wondered if they'd have chosen his library design in the first place if they'd known he was gay. In the end, he'd decided it didn't matter. He wasn't going to change who he was, so the business world could go to hell if they didn't like it.

"There're other jobs," he said, releasing Bobbi. He just hoped he could get one in Chicago. With Nash's softball season starting soon and Luke's recent move to the city, the last thing Sidney wanted was to relocate.

A company security guard stepped into the large open room and made his way towards Sidney's small work area. "You'd better go," he told Bobbi.

After a teary-eyed Bobbi wandered back to her own drawing table, Sidney began the process of packing up. He wrapped the few framed photos he had in paper towels swiped from the restroom and a few other supplies that he'd purchased himself.

Sidney pointed towards the large crock of pencils and pens. "Is it okay if I take these or do they plan to reuse them?" he asked the guard.

"I'm just here to make sure you don't try to take any of the company's blueprints," the guard informed him.

"Cool." Sidney grabbed the crock and put the entire thing in the box. Within moments, there was no trace that he'd sat in the same location for the last three and a half years. He slung his messenger bag over his shoulder and picked up the box.

It wasn't until he made his way out of the building that depression started to kick in. Although he knew he'd made the right choice, it sucked to realise how easily he could be replaced.

* * * *

Nash was surprised to arrive home and see Sidney's car in the driveway. "Hello?" he called, shutting the front door. He quickly took off his boots and set them beside the entry table.

"In here," Sidney answered from the kitchen.

Nash pulled off his dirty T-shirt before making his way to the kitchen. "Something smells good. Is that Swiss steak?" He gave Sidney a kiss on the neck before taking a seat at the table.

Dressed in his bathrobe, Sidney covered the skillet on the stove and opened the refrigerator. "Yep. I was hoping you wouldn't stop off at Wally's."

"You could've called the garage to let me know you were home," Nash replied, taking the offered ice cold bottle of beer.

"I didn't want to put you in an awkward position." Sidney pulled a small tube of lube from his pocket. "I'd like to sit on your lap, but there are way too many clothes in the way."

Nash's brows shot up. It had been a while since Sidney had felt like kitchen sex. "Something going on?" he asked, unzipping his jeans.

Sidney waited until Nash was completely naked before untying the robe and climbing on to Nash's lap. "I quit my job today," he announced.

Nash took a deep breath. Suddenly it all made sense. Sidney was feeling insecure and needed sex to feel safe. "Why'd you quit?" he asked, taking the lube from Sidney.

"They wanted me to work a job in Saudi Arabia. When I refused, I was given the choice to quit or be terminated."

Although Sidney said it in a matter-of-fact fashion, Nash could tell there was a hell of a lot more to the story. He took his time, lubing his fingers before reaching under the robe to the crack of Sidney's ass. "And they just sprang this on you today?"

Sidney bit his bottom lip, eventually shaking his head. "My boss mentioned it a couple months ago, but I wasn't officially given the offer until yesterday."

Nash stopped in the process of inserting his middle finger into Sidney's hole. "And you didn't say anything about it? Don't you think we should've at least discussed it?"

Leaning his forehead against Nash's shoulder, Sidney shook his head again. "It wasn't an option, in my opinion. There's no way we could've gone there together, not with the laws the way they are there, and I wasn't about to go on my own."

Nash was angry that he hadn't been let in on the decision, but he understood Sidney's position. He concentrated on preparing Sidney's body for his cock while he tried to calm himself. It didn't help matters that the majority of their savings were currently tied up in the stock market. Neither did the fact that he was almost ready to discuss the possibility of quitting his job at the garage and working the market on a full-time basis. Of course, that would have to be put on hold for the time being. At least until Sidney could find another job.

"I'm sorry," Sidney whispered, kissing Nash's neck.

"It's not your fault, babe." Nash removed his fingers and ran his slicked hand over his cock. He held it by the base and waited for Sidney to take him in.

"I'll go out tomorrow and start looking for another one," Sidney promised, lowering himself on Nash's length.

Once Sidney was fully seated, Nash grabbed the back of Sidney's hair and pulled his head back. "I don't ever want you to feel you can't come to me with a problem."

"I don't know why I didn't tell you. I guess I was embarrassed that a company I'd given my all to would push me against a wall like that."

"I don't want you to rush out and get another job if it means working for assholes like that again. Take your time. The right job will come along eventually. In the meantime, I've got your back."

"You always have," Sidney moaned as he started to move up and down on Nash's cock.

* * * *

Sidney looked at the scrap of paper in his hand to check the address once more before entering the old brick building. Other than the address, there were no signs out front to tell him the tiny building was the home of Creative Solutions.

A bell sounded as Sidney stepped inside. He was immediately impressed with his surroundings. Despite the apparent age of the structure and its limited size, the interior was both modern and classic.

"May I help you?" a woman asked, coming around the corner with a toddler in her arms.

"Yes, I hope so. I have an appointment with Ben Shriver." Sidney held his breath, hoping he had the right place.

The woman smiled. "You must be Sidney." She set the little boy on his feet and held out her hand. "I'm Abby Shriver, Ben's wife." She gestured to the boy who continued to eat a bag of snack crackers. "And this is BJ."

"Nice to meet you both."

"Ben's on the phone, but he should be finished soon. Can I get you something to drink while you wait?"

Sidney shook his head. "No, thanks." He gestured to the exposed overhead beams. "How's that possible with the Chicago weather the way it is?"

Abby's face lit up with pride. "Because my husband's a genius. I'll let him tell you how he managed to accomplish it. But just so you know, its toasty warm in here in the winter and cool in the summer."

Sidney couldn't wait to meet the man who inspired such devotion in a partner. "I'll be sure and ask him."

"Ask me what?" a handsome man enquired, coming into the room.

"Sidney wants to know how you managed to keep the exposed beams and rafters," Abby informed him.

The man stepped forward and held out his hand. "Ben Shriver, it's a pleasure to meet you."

Sidney shook Ben's hand. "This whole place is amazing. Did you remodel it yourself?"

Ben chuckled. "My ideas, but my brothers did the actual construction." Ben waved Sidney towards the partitioned off area. "Step into my office."

"I'm heading out," Abby said before they could leave the room. She gave Ben a quick kiss before picking up BJ and holding him out for Ben to kiss. "It was nice meeting you, Sidney. I hope you say yes to the offer so I can have my husband back," she said with a giggle before leaving.

Sidney followed Ben behind the ten-foot partition to a large, open work room with floor to ceiling windows. "Nice," he commented.

"Thanks." Ben sat at an oval table and gestured for Sidney to take a seat. "I have to tell you, I was more than shocked that you answered the ad in the paper. I wasn't expecting someone with your qualifications to be interested in a one-man operation like mine. I can't tell you how many times I've gone to the library you designed just to sit in awe of the structure itself."

Pride filled Sidney. He'd fielded offers from several large architectural firms in Chicago but none of them had felt right. The last thing he wanted was to be put in the same position again that had caused him to leave Miles, McShane and Frawling.

When he'd run across the small help-wanted ad from Creative Solutions the Highland Park address had appealed to him more than anything else, but now seeing the building and meeting Ben and his family only cemented his decision to give Creative Solutions a shot. "I live just down the road in Lake Forest," he told Ben. "Thought it might be nice to get home in time to eat dinner at a decent hour."

"I can understand that. Since business has started to pick up, I can't remember the last time I had a real dinner with my family." Ben leaned his forearms on the table. "Before we get into the meagre salary I can afford at the moment, let me tell you a little about the company."

"Sounds good," Sidney agreed.

"Right now, Creative Solutions specialises in retrofitting old buildings to meet the needs of today's clients." He pointed towards the rafters. "In a space like this, the charm comes from the old. The problem is, as you noticed, insulation issues. Although the solution wasn't inexpensive, I think it was worth it. What we did was to basically build another roofline on top of the original, leaving plenty of space for insulation and airflow. If you look closely from the outside of the building you can tell it's higher, but from inside you'd never know."

Sidney continued to stare up at the exposed beams as Ben explained the process he'd used. "Fantastic." It was that kind of creative thinking he wanted to be a part of. Sidney's arms broke out in gooseflesh at the prospect.

"I'm glad you think so. The job's yours if you want it, because right now I could definitely use your help. My brothers own Shriver's Construction Company, one of the biggest in the region, and they've been contracted for a job that isn't in my area of expertise."

Sidney leant forward in his excitement. "What kind of project?"

"This particular client seems to have more money than sense, but that's beside the point. He wants a castle built on a piece of land he's recently purchased. Since my area of design is more centred on refurbishing existing structures, I need someone creative who can start from scratch. That's where you'd come in."

"I'll do it!" Sidney shouted, a tad too enthusiastically.

Ben chuckled. "I'm glad you're excited by the project, but you might want to know how much I can pay you before you jump on it."

"Will I make enough to live on with a couple extra bucks to put into savings at the end of the month?" Sidney asked.

"I think we can work something out," Ben agreed.

"Good. Then I only have one more concern to address." Sidney knew it was the biggest concern of all. He prayed Ben was as open-minded as he appeared.

"Okay, shoot."

"I'm a gay man with a partner whom I love very much. I need to know I won't be subjected to harassment by you or anyone else I'll be working with on a regular basis."

Ben shook his head. "No worries there. Of course, I can't speak for the individual clients who'll come and go, but I've got a brother who's gay, so no one in the family will treat you any differently because of it."

Satisfied, Sidney stood and extended his hand. "If the offer's still open, I'll take it."

* * * *

June 1994

After a drive into the city to pick up Luke, Sidney headed towards the ball field. "I still can't believe I'm going to finally get to see Nash play ball."

"What's been the problem up until now?" Luke asked, flipping through radio stations.

Sidney bit his bottom lip and tried to come up with something that wouldn't make Luke think less of Nash. "It's Nash's work team."

"And?"

"He's not out at the garage," he mumbled under his breath.

When Luke said nothing in reply, Sidney eventually glanced towards his passenger. "What?"

Luke shook his head. "What is it about the jackasses at that garage that cause grown-ass men to be afraid to be who they are?"

"You talking about Butch?"

"I can tell he likes me, but he keeps me at arm's length. I thought it was the chair, but now that you said that about the garage, I'm wondering if that's the problem."

"I think you're right about him being in to you, but I also think Butch has issues and not just about coming out to the guys at the garage."

They rode in silence for several miles before Luke cleared his throat. "He kissed me, ya know?"

There was something so innocent in Luke's voice that Sidney couldn't help but smile. "And was it a good one?"

Luke turned bright red.

"Ooh, that good or that bad?" Sidney could tell by the flush creeping up Luke's neck it had been the former, but he wanted Luke to admit it.

"It was only one kiss, but it was the most consuming act I've ever experienced. I swear to God the man kisses with his entire body." Luke's upper body gave a dramatic shiver.

"Then we'd better make sure we get you some more of that Butch-kind of loving," Sidney said around a laugh.

"I'm all ears," Luke replied.

"Let me think about it, and I'll get back to you." Sidney pulled into the sports complex and parked two spaces away from Butch's Harley. "Just don't get offended if Butch ignores you today. I don't even know if *he knows* we're coming."

* * * *

Butch slapped Nash's thigh with his glove. "Do you think Sidney needs help getting the chair out of the trunk?"

Nash followed Butch's line of sight and landed on his gorgeous partner, struggling with the heavy wheelchair. "Yeah, why don't you run over and save the day, Captain America."

Butch shoved his ball glove against Nash's torso a little harder than was necessary. "Smart-ass."

Nash watched as Butch sprinted over and easily lifted the chair out of the small trunk. Deciding to join the three men, Nash glanced at the rest of the team who were busy warming up. He still wasn't sure if he was ready to alienate half the men he worked with, but he'd done a lot of soul-searching after Sidney had been forced to give up his job with Miles, McShane and Frawling.

It didn't matter that Sidney was happier than he'd ever seen him in his new job. The fact that Sidney had walked away from a prestigious job out of love for Nash had been more than enough to convince Nash it was time to do the right thing. "Glad you could make it," Nash said to Luke before brushing a quick kiss across Sidney's lips.

Sidney's eyes rounded in surprise. "You didn't have to do that."

"Yeah I did." Nash let Butch and Luke travel a short distance ahead of them before he spoke again. "You're more important to me than any damn job. If they make it too unbearable, like you I'll quit and find something else."

Sidney brushed his shoulder against Nash. "That's sweet, but I know how much your friends mean to you."

"See, that's the thing. I used to get so damn mad at Butch because he refused to open up about himself, but I realised I've been doing the same thing. Maybe not with him, but with everyone else."

Sidney nodded. "But there's a difference between being honest with people and shoving it in their faces." He gestured towards the parking lot. "I didn't need a kiss back there. Hell, you fucked me not two hours ago. Let's just play it cool when we're around them. I'm good with that."

Nash smiled. "Thanks."

* * * *

After the game the team made their way to Wally's. Sidney sat between Nash and Luke with Butch on Luke's other side. "Good game," Sidney told Nash again.

"Yeah it was. We kicked their asses," Butch said with a whoop.

The surrounding teammates sent up a cheer of their own at Butch's comment. Sidney glanced at Luke. He'd been hesitant about inviting Luke to the game; worried the man would become depressed. Although it had been years since Luke had been physically able to play sports, the expression on his face told Sidney that Luke hadn't forgotten the feeling of team camaraderie.

"Luke played baseball for the University of Pittsburgh," Sidney told Butch once the cheers had died down.

"You were a Panther?" Butch asked, sounding surprised.

"Three years," Luke answered with pride in his voice. "I was on full-ride."

Butch whistled. "I'm impressed. I grew up in Cleveland. Went to Ohio State for a few years." As if someone had flipped a switch on his mood, Butch suddenly became sullen. "Excuse me." Butch pushed himself away from the table and headed for the restroom.

"Is he okay?" Luke asked.

Not knowing Butch well enough, Sidney deferred to Nash. "Maybe you should check on him."

Nash rose with a sigh. "He'll either talk or punch my face in."

"Hopefully it's the former," Sidney replied, brushing his hand against Nash's leg.

Nash strode to the restroom, wondering if it had been a mistake to invite Luke along. Since Thanksgiving, Butch had seemed a lot moodier than normal. He knocked on the door before pushing it open. "Butch?"

"Jesus! Can't I go to the bathroom without you following me?" Butch yelled.

Nash leaned against the stall door. "Luke wanted me to make sure you were okay."

"I'm fine. I'm always...fine."

Nash knew Butch wasn't telling the truth. Instead of accusing his friend of lying, Nash decided to head in a different direction. "I didn't know you'd gone to Ohio State."

"Yeah, well I don't tell you everything."

"That's for damn sure. Why'd you leave?" Nash was pushing and he knew it, but it was a chance to learn

121

something about Butch, and he wasn't about to let it pass him by.

The stall door opened, and Nash was thrown off balance. Butch caught him before he was able to hit the ground. "Why're you so damn nosey?" Butch asked, resettling Nash on his feet.

Nash took a deep breath. "Because I love you. I wasn't bullshitting when I told you that, outside of Sidney, you're the best friend I've ever had. I can tell you're in pain, but I don't know how to help."

"I'm not in pain, doctor, so drop it."

Nash shook his head. "Not this time. Tell me why you left college?"

Butch turned and punched the stall door, creating a large dent in the metal. "Because I was stupid enough to think I could be myself there and someone died because of it. Okay!"

Nash noticed the blood on Butch's knuckles and gently led him over to the sink. He didn't speak right away, concentrating on running cold water over the split knuckle. "A boyfriend?"

"Not really. I mean, it was only our third date."

"What happened?"

Butch shrugged. "Some folks didn't like seeing two dudes holding hands, I guess. Jumped us as we were walking home from a movie. Johnny died from a blow to the head with a tire iron."

Nash tried to swallow. "Fuck."

Butch pulled his hand away and reached for a paper towel. "I was so taken off guard that I couldn't even identify the fucker in a police line-up. Johnny died and I couldn't even bring his killer to justice."

Nash was at a loss as to what to say. He tried to put himself in Butch's position, but quickly shoved the image of Sidney bleeding to death away. "I...I don't..."

"Yeah. You don't have to say anything. There's nothing to say that could make me feel better anyway. It's why I never told you."

"Is it the reason you don't date?"

"Yep. I still fuck, but only people I don't give a shit about. Nameless guys I pick up in bars. It's easier that way."

"And lonelier," Nash added.

"My cross to bear and all that." Butch dabbed the paper towel against his knuckle to stop the bleeding. "I really don't want to talk about this anymore."

"I know." He thought about what Sidney had whispered to him earlier in the afternoon. "Luke really likes you. And I kinda think both of you deserve some happiness in your lives."

"What kind of a friend are you? Do you really want to put Luke in that kind of a position?" Butch asked, throwing away the paper towel.

Nash shook his head. "I wasn't there that night, so I don't know the details, but I'm confident that you would've stopped it if you could have." Nash put a hand on Butch's shoulder. "I have faith that you would do everything in your power to keep Luke safe."

"Exactly what I'm doing by leaving him alone," Butch countered.

"So you're willing to take the chance of Luke finding someone else who won't take as good of care of him as you could?" Nash waited, knowing his question would cause a reaction.

Butch's nostrils flared. "I'd kill anyone who tried to hurt him."

"I know. Which is why I think he needs you. We both know Chicago isn't the easiest city to live in. Can you imagine navigating it in a wheelchair without the ability to run away from trouble?"

Butch's forehead furrowed. Without another word, he turned and strode out of the restroom. Nash hoped he'd done the right thing. Butch could be intense at times. Hopefully Luke knew what he was getting into because Nash doubted Butch was the kind of man who'd walk away from something, or someone, once he'd made up his mind.

* * * *

After showering the dirt and sweat from his body, Nash entered the bedroom with a towel wrapped around his waist. "I heard Butch mumbling something about needing to get a car. You think it could have something to do with Luke?"

Sidney lowered the magazine he was reading just as Nash ripped off his towel. Lord have mercy, the man was fine. "Hope so." He threw the covers off his naked body, exposing himself to Nash's gaze. "Luke wants Butch as much as I want you."

"Really?" Nash used the towel to rub the water from his hair. "And how much is that?"

Sidney tossed his magazine to the floor and rolled over, sticking his ass in the air. "Enough to beg, given half a chance." He looked over his shoulder at Nash. "Do you want me to beg? Because I will."

Nash neared the bed, stopping only long enough to retrieve the lube. "When's the last time I made you beg?"

Sidney tapped his chin with his finger. "Let's see, I seem to recall the first night you kissed me under the

Christmas tree. If I'm not mistaken, I'd have done anything to get your cock in me."

Nash knelt behind Sidney and ran his tongue back and forth across his puckered hole before sitting back on his heels. He opened the lube and let several drops slide down the crack of Sidney's ass, using his fingers to smear it over his hole. "But once I finally gave in to my desire there was no going back for me."

"Liar. I seem to recall you sending me back to school with a broken heart."

Although Sidney was in a playful mood, the reminder cut Nash like a knife. It had been the biggest mistake of Nash's life. If he'd have been honest with himself about his feelings for Sidney the car accident would never have happened. "Yeah," he finally mumbled.

"Shit." Sidney rolled over and sat up to face Nash. "I'm sorry. I shouldn't have brought it up."

"It's okay."

"No, it's not." Sidney pulled Nash down on top of him. "I've known you for twenty years and, in all that time, I can count on one hand the times you let me down. I know you tend to dwell on the bad times, but there aren't enough fingers in Chicago to count the good times I've had since meeting you."

Nash leaned in for a kiss, thrusting his tongue deep into Sidney's mouth. He knew he'd always think of the times he'd let Sidney down. How else would he keep himself from making the same mistakes twice? No matter what, he'd always be there to love and support Sidney.

Nash ground his hardened cock against Sidney. "I love you."

"I love you, too," Sidney whispered, wrapping his legs around Nash's waist.

As Nash closed in on Sidney's mouth for a deep kiss, he couldn't help but wonder how the guys at work would treat him come Monday morning. Then he sank his cock into Sidney's heated body, and realised he didn't give a damn. All he needed to be happy was the man underneath him, a job he enjoyed and a few good friends. The rest of the world could go to hell if they didn't approve.

FALL

Dedication

To the men and women who love each other
enough to get through the hard times without
giving up.

Chapter One

November 1996

Sidney arrived home just as his phone rang. He set down his messenger bag and reached for it. "Hello?"

"Is this Sidney Wilks?" a woman's voice asked.

"Yes." Sidney prepared to hang up. Calls from people trying to sell him bullshit were starting to get out of control.

"This is Sheila, Jackson's wife. I thought you should know your father had a massive stroke yesterday morning."

"Is he dead?" It was the only thing going through Sidney's mind. He'd become so detached from his estranged father, he often went weeks without even thinking about the bastard. The fact that Sheila, a stepmother he'd never even met, was calling, didn't bode well.

"No. Not yet anyway, but the doctors believe it's only a matter of time. This was his third stroke in the last year and his body's just not able to handle much more. He's at North Colorado Medical Center."

Sidney remained silent. He had no intention of travelling to Colorado, especially with Thanksgiving only two days away. Did that make him a bastard? Probably. But Sidney believed strongly in the old saying, you reap what you sow.

Sheila cleared her throat. It was obvious she'd been crying, and although Sidney felt no love for the woman, he was still human. "Are you okay?" he finally asked.

"Not really," she answered. "I know the two of you haven't spoken for years, but he's still your father. You may not remember that but he does."

"Does he? How long were the two of you married before he actually told you he had a queer son?" Sidney took a deep breath. Yelling at a distraught woman wasn't going to solve anything. Few outsiders would understand Sidney's contempt for Jackson Wilks.

"We've had our issues over your father's secrecy, but that's all in the past now."

"Is it?" Sidney silently cursed himself for trying to pick a fight with a distraught woman. "Thank you for calling, Sheila. Let me know if there are any changes."

"Is that all?" she asked.

"Yeah. That's the best I can do for now. Sorry." Sidney hung up before dropping onto the sofa.

He was still sitting in the same spot when his partner of twelve years, Grady Nash, walked into the house from his office in the detached garage. Sidney smiled up at the man he loved. "Dad's had a stroke."

"Shit." Nash sank down onto the couch and wrapped an arm around Sidney. "Who called?"

"Sheila. I guess Dad finally decided to tell her about me. The fact that she hadn't bothered calling before now to introduce herself tells me everything I need to know about her feelings." For over an hour Sidney had been trying to pull some kind of emotion out of himself with no luck. He leaned against Nash's chest and closed his eyes. "She pretty much said he wouldn't recover from this one."

Nash kissed the top of Sidney's head. "Are you going to see him?"

Sidney shook his head. "I've got Thanksgiving dinner to prepare in two days, and I still haven't finished the grocery shopping."

"You know none of that matters if you want to go, right?"

"They matter to me. I won't slight the Ballentines to run off to Colorado to see a man who never loved me just because he's dying. Or to meet a family who've never acknowledged my existence."

Nash sat back and tilted Sidney's chin up. "That's not true. Jackson may be a self-centred asshole, but he did love you. I'm not gonna sit here and try to defend his actions because they still make me sick to my stomach to think about, but just because he didn't seem to like you doesn't mean he didn't have feelings for you."

Sidney stared up at Nash. Where someone who didn't know Nash as well as he did would think the man was sticking up for Jackson, Sidney knew the truth. Put simply, Nash didn't want Sidney to believe his own father was incapable of loving him. "You've always been my champion," he whispered, reaching up to cup Nash's face. "If he holds on until after the holidays, I'll think about it."

Nash pulled Sidney into a deep kiss. Sidney opened immediately and accepted the silent comfort with ease. Even if his father died before the holiday, Sidney would never regret time spent with the people he loved.

* * * *

Butch dropped Luke off at Sidney's before heading out once more. Sidney shut the door and turned to his friend. "How'd you get out of going to the airport?"

Luke wheeled himself over to the end table beside the sofa. "He needed the space in the trunk for luggage." He grabbed a handful of M&M's from a glass bowl. After popping all of them into his mouth, he flashed Sidney a devilish grin. "Besides, I enjoy making him squirm. It'll be the first time he's alone with my family."

"You're cruel," Sidney reminded his friend.

"Yep. Payback for making me work so damn hard to get him to commit."

It had been almost two years since Butch had confessed his feelings for Luke, but it had taken another year and a half for Butch to agree to live with him. Sidney grinned. Butch had been helping move Sidney and Nash into their new house. When Luke hadn't shown up to help, Butch had started to worry. After an hour of calling Luke's phone without an answer, Butch had taken off towards the city. Finding out Luke had fallen getting out of the shower had cemented Butch's decision. The two of them moved into a house together two months later.

Shaking his head, Sidney walked to the kitchen. "Come and help me peel potatoes."

"Sure, make the guy in the wheelchair do all the dirty work," Luke mumbled, following Sidney.

"You can always go in and vacuum the media room if you'd rather do that," Sidney fired back.

"Give me the fucking potatoes," Luke grumbled, pulling up to the kitchen table.

Sidney sat a ten pound bag of potatoes on the table in front of Luke along with a paring knife, pan and bowl for the peelings. "There you go."

Luke held up the knife. "Are you so country that you don't have a damn potato peeler?"

Sidney rolled his eyes and removed a peeler from the back of the utility drawer. "Sorry, I thought I was working with an adult, not a twelve-year-old."

"Whatever." Luke took the peeler and started in on the potatoes. "So, have you heard anything on your dad?"

Sidney paused in the middle of checking the pumpkin pies in the oven. "No." Evidently he'd been such an ass to Sheila that she hadn't bothered to call back. Nash had been on Sidney to give the hospital a call, but Sidney couldn't bring himself to do it. "As far as I know he's still alive."

"Do you think maybe he's changed? I know my grandpa Maxwell was different after his stroke. He was more than a bastard before it happened, but suddenly he was this old man who seemed to get all emotional over the tiniest thing."

Sidney shut the oven door. "He's got three other kids now. I doubt he's missing the fag of the family."

Luke glanced over his shoulder before turning back to his work. "My folks have a house full of kids and despite everything Josh has put them through, it would kill them if they thought he felt that way."

"Yeah, well, your parents are different."

Luke shook his head. "I'm sure Josh would say the same as you just did. That's the thing though. Just because you believe it, doesn't make it true."

Nash walked into the kitchen, whistling. "Hey," he greeted Luke before stopping to give Sidney a kiss. "The tables and chairs are all set up, but I could only find three of the four tablecloths."

Sidney leaned against Nash, wishing he had time for a nap. "Did you check the sack that has the candles? It might've gotten shoved in there at the store."

"What sack is that?" Nash asked.

"The one I handed you earlier?"

Nash's brows drew together. "Right. Umm, I'll have to look."

Sidney smiled. "You have no idea where you put that sack, do you?"

Nash grinned. "Not really, but I'll find it." He gave Sidney another kiss, this one much deeper than the first. "Everything else in here going according to schedule?"

Luke sent out a bark of laughter. "Evidently not or he wouldn't have the guest peeling potatoes."

"Shut up and peel. I need to get those on the stove," Sidney ordered, somehow managing to keep a straight face.

"You see how he treats me?" Luke asked.

"Yep. Like one of the family," Nash observed. He gave Sidney's ass a squeeze before leaving the kitchen.

"He's right, you know," Sidney said after Nash left. "I love you like the brother I never wanted."

"Fucker," Luke chuckled. "I would've stayed in Pennsylvania if I wanted this kind of abuse."

"But then you wouldn't have met Mr Lovey-Dovey Muscle Man."

Luke's entire expression softened. "You're right. I guess it's worth putting up with your abuse after all."

"Damn straight."

* * * *

Nash opened the front door and the Ballentine crew poured into the house. He shook hands with Alan while Sidney was swept up in a hug by Maggie before moving to the next guest. "How was the flight?" he asked Peter, his mentor and new business partner.

"Fine, except I had to sit next to Zac." Peter shook his head. "If he wasn't snoring, he was talking about pussy."

Nash gave a dramatic shiver. "I'm glad I'm not you."

Peter glanced over his shoulder at Sidney. "I guess not." He chuckled and reached down to pat Nash's stomach with the back of his hand. "You'd better lay off the beer."

Nash played off the gesture, but glanced down after Peter had moved further into the room. Since leaving the garage, he'd packed on a few pounds, but he didn't realise it was so noticeable. Hell, he was a forty-year-old day trader, what did people expect?

"Can you hang these on that rack I put up in the laundry room?" Sidney asked, dumping a load of coats in Nash's arms.

"Sure."

Another coat landed on the pile before Nash could get out of the room. Zac's bomber jacket smelt like a combination of leather, cologne and perfume. Nash wondered if Zac even knew the name of the woman whose perfumed scent still followed him. The youngest of the Ballentine brothers, Zac, was an up and coming advertising executive. Although he wasn't as handsome as Luke, Zac had the playful personality that seemed to draw the women in like bears to honey.

Nash set the coats on the washing machine and reached for a hanger. As he hung up the coats, one by one, he realised how much a coat said about a person. Peter's Burberry trench coat was functional, expensive and boring. Alan's cashmere coat probably cost more than a house payment, but it was truly an object of understated wealth and elegance. Nash grinned when he hung up Maggie's puffy down coat. Just like Maggie—all business—whatever it took to get the job done.

Nash was smiling by the time he walked out of the laundry room, the remark about his weight forgotten. He entered the kitchen and embraced the loud voices trying to talk over each other. It was another year of being surrounded by the people who'd become like family to him.

"Did you get that email I sent?" Peter asked, pouring a cup of coffee.

"Yeah. I sent the information to Don this morning," he replied. His online trading job had taken off to include a small consulting company with Peter. Nash didn't like giving others advice on stocks nearly as much as actually taking the gamble for himself, but it had been a great source of income. "Sorry Janet couldn't come with you."

Peter was quiet for a moment. "I'm not. We needed the time."

It was the first wrinkle Nash had seen in Peter's perfect life. "Trouble?"

Peter glanced around the room before continuing. "I think she's having an affair," he said, low enough for Nash's ears only.

"So you just left her back in Philadelphia? Do you really think she's going to spend the next three days alone?" Nash didn't understand people. If he thought Sidney was dallying on the side he'd be stuck to his man like glue, twenty-four-seven.

"Thing is, I don't really care." Peter shrugged. "I think our marriage has run its course."

Granted it had been six months since he'd seen Peter and Janet together, but they'd always seemed like the perfect couple. Although they were both wrapped up in their individual careers, the two seemed to dote on each other. The news of trouble knocked Nash on his ass. "I'm sorry to hear that."

Peter held the coffee cup in front of his mouth, periodically blowing on the hot java. "Yeah, we're lucky Janet never could get pregnant. Can you imagine how messy a custody battle would be between the two of us?"

Nash looked at his friend as if seeing him for the first time. *Lucky?* He wasn't sure what exactly had happened to destroy the once happy couple, but Nash knew for a fact Peter had wanted children. "Is there another woman?"

"There're always other women, but, no, I haven't met anyone else. I just don't have the time or the energy to deal with the bullshit anymore."

Nash knew he was about to step on toes, but he couldn't keep quiet. "With an attitude like that, I can see why Janet might've gone elsewhere."

Peter narrowed his eyes and sat his coffee cup in the sink. "Back off. You're my business partner, not my shrink."

"You're right, I'm not." Nash left Peter standing in the kitchen and sought out Sidney. He was troubled more than he cared to admit and needed the smile of the one man he could always count on to make him feel better.

Sidney was in the garage fussing with the centre pieces with Luke and Butch looking on. "Looks pretty," Nash said, wrapping his arms around Sidney from behind.

"It's okay. Not my best, but not bad for an amateur." Sidney turned and gave Nash a hug. "Everything okay?"

"Yeah. Just needed to see your smiling face." Looking into Sidney's big brown eyes, Nash couldn't imagine a life without the love shining back at him. "Love you."

Sidney looked confused for a moment before he smiled once more. "I love you, too."

"Are you gonna make out?" Butch asked.

Nash turned to his friend who had a beer in one hand and Luke's thigh in the other. "Why, you wanna watch?"

"No. I was hoping you'd get me another beer," Butch answered.

Luke leaned over and gave Butch a quick kiss on the lips. "You can get one yourself when you go back into the house with me to talk to my family."

"Do I have to?" Butch asked.

Luke pulled the top of Butch's bald head down and kissed it. "Yep. Unless you'd rather sleep on the blow-up mattress tonight."

Butch stood and shook his head. "You play dirty pool."

"I know," Luke agreed as Butch pushed him out of the garage.

Alone with Sidney, Nash let his hands wander down to the sweet ass he loved. "Do we have time for a quickie?"

"I wish." Sidney ground his erection against Nash's thigh. "Unfortunately, I have a turkey to get out of the oven, potatoes to mash and gravy to make."

Although Sidney made a show of listing off what he still had yet to do, Nash knew the truth was a different story. "You love this stuff, don't you?"

"Yeah, a little bit." Sidney tickled Nash's chin with the tip of his tongue. "Will you be able to do without my ass for another six or seven hours?"

"Don't have much choice. No other ass I want, so I'll wait for yours." He released Sidney after delving in for a deep kiss. "You'd better get to work."

"Will you tell me later what's bothering you?" Sidney asked.

"That depends on whether or not I'm still letting it bother me."

* * * *

With Zac in one guest room and Peter in the other, Sidney finally gave up the fight to stay awake and entered the master bedroom. Nash, as usual, was leaning back against the headboard, typing away on his laptop. He didn't bother asking how the market was doing, he never understood it anyway. A drop of twenty cents seemed to send Nash into a tailspin but it was just twenty cents to Sidney.

Sidney collapsed on the bed with his clothes on and sighed. "What a day."

Nash tapped a few keys before closing the laptop. He tossed back the covers, exposing his nude body before carrying the computer to the dresser. "It certainly was." He stood over Sidney with his hands on his hips. "You need me to undress you?"

Sidney's eyes wandered down Nash's body, enjoying the view. "I should probably shower." Although he was too tired to fuck, Sidney could tell by Nash's filling cock that his partner planned to make good on their earlier conversation.

Nash pulled off Sidney's socks before unzipping his jeans. "You can take one in the morning." He eased Sidney's jeans down and off, taking a moment to nuzzle Sidney's balls with his face.

Although Sidney was tired, his cock took notice of the attention. With his sweater halfway off, Sidney started backing up towards his pillow. "Come hold me."

Nash draped the sweater over a chair in the corner of the room before pouncing on the bed. He pulled Sidney against his chest and wrapped his arms around him. "You should've taken Maggie up on her offer to help you more than you did."

"Yeah, like she lets me help when I'm at her house. I'm lucky if she lets me dry the dishes." Sidney licked Nash's nipple, teasing the protruding nub with the tip of his tongue. "My mind wants to fuck but my body wants to sleep." He ran his hand down Nash's chest, stopping to circle the slight paunch of the man he loved.

Nash's body stiffened at the gesture and quickly pushed Sidney's hand lower, towards his cock. "Don't. You wanna play with something, play with that."

The defensive tone of Nash's voice bothered Sidney. "I wasn't playing." He leaned up to look Nash in the eyes. "What's going on?"

"Peter thinks I'm getting fat."

"Fat?" Sidney shook his head. "You've got a bit of a belly, but you're getting older and you're not as active as you used to be. Screw Peter and what he thinks." He brushed a kiss across Nash's lips. "You're still the sexiest man I've ever known."

Nash didn't appear to be convinced. He pulled Sidney back down and snuggled against him. "Get some sleep. We've got guests to make brunch for in the morning."

With the cock in his hand now flaccid, Sidney knew Nash was no longer in the mood for sex. From experience, Sidney knew it would only take a quick blowjob to get Nash interested again, but he was tired and the moment had passed. "I love you just the way you are," he whispered.

When Nash didn't reply to the statement, Sidney squeezed his eyes shut. He promised himself he'd start paying more attention to the food he put on the table. It wasn't all Nash's fault he was gaining weight. Sidney had been lax in cooking healthy dinners lately, opting instead to stop by somewhere on the way home and get takeout.

The moment the holidays were over, Sidney would do whatever it took to make sure Nash had something healthy to eat on the dinner table every night.

* * * *

The after-Thanksgiving brunch had become a bigger affair than the actual holiday meal. Not only did it include the Ballentine clan but friends from the area who had spent Thanksgiving with their own families.

Nash and Butch stared at the table configuration in the mock dining room. "I think we need a bigger house," Nash determined.

"Or a bigger garage. *Or* fewer guests," Butch added.

Nash glanced up at his friend. "How's it going at your place?" He knew from Butch's grumblings before the Ballentines arrived that having Luke's family in the house wasn't something he was comfortable with.

"Let's just say Luke was right to move away from them. They treat him like a fucking baby. Hell, he was folding a load of towels yesterday and Maggie gave me a look that could kill. They were *towels* for fuck sake."

"She loves him." Nash shrugged. "Maggie's never said it, but I think he's always been her favourite."

"He's my favourite too, but I sure as hell don't put him in a corner and expect him to stay there." Butch ran a hand over his bald head. "Maybe it's the mother thing I don't get. Lord knows I never had someone who cared enough to hover."

The door opened and Luke wheeled into the garage. "Thought I might find you out here." He reached for the steaming, fragrant brew in the cup holder attached to the frame of his chair. "Figured you could use some coffee." Luke grinned at Nash. "Sorry, only one holder."

Nash slapped Butch on the back as he reached for the coffee. "I think you have someone who cares enough to hover."

"I'm not hovering," Luke denied. "I just happen to know Butch only had one cup this morning before we left the house."

Nash chuckled. "Okay, maybe not hovering, but you definitely dote on him."

Luke looked Butch up and down, eating the man with his gaze. "Who wouldn't?"

"See? It's just a sexual thing," Butch said. "Luke's obsessed with my body."

"So you think he brings you coffee because he wants your cock?" Nash asked.

Luke suddenly looked guilty. "Actually, I was kinda hoping he'd be alone out here."

"Told ya." Butch ran his fingers through Luke's short hair. "He can't seem to get enough of me."

"Or, it could have something to do with the fact you made us both sleep in pyjamas last night," Luke countered. He looked up at Nash. "He wouldn't even let me give him a handjob. Prude."

"Your parents were in the next room," Butch argued.

Nash wasn't sure who he felt the most sorry for. He gestured to the office attached to the back of the garage. "My office has a lock on it. I'm going to go help Sidney in the kitchen."

Butch took a sip of his coffee before sitting it down on the table. "See ya in twenty minutes," he told Nash, wheeling Luke towards the closed door.

One glance at the erection pressing against the front of Butch's jeans and Nash knew otherwise. "Probably ten." He hightailed it out of the garage before Butch could reach him, feeling better than he had all morning.

Chapter Two

After a celebratory birthday dinner out with friends, Nash draped a blanket over the upholstery and stretched out on the couch while Sidney puttered around in the kitchen. "What're you doing in there? Come on, old man. I'm ready to watch a movie."

He stared at the VHS tapes arranged on the coffee table and reached for his cock. It had become a tradition, of sorts, to spend Sidney's birthday fucking and watching porn, and Nash wanted to get started.

Sidney sauntered into the room wearing the short black robe Nash had given him for Christmas. "I had to get stuff." He unloaded his arms, setting lube, two bottles of water and frosting on the table.

Nash stared at the can of fudge frosting. Since Thanksgiving he'd been on a strict diet, going as far as to give up his evenings at the bar with his friends so he wouldn't be tempted to drink beer. "I'm not eating that."

Sidney glanced over his shoulder, away from the video tapes. "It's my birthday. We didn't have cake, but I thought we could at least play with frosting. You've barely eaten enough to keep a bird alive lately, I hoped you could splurge."

Nash pulled Sidney into his arms, slipping his hand under the robe to brush against a nipple. "How about I let you lick it off me, and I'll sing the birthday song while you do it?"

Sidney leaned his head against Nash's chest and sighed. "I know how hard you've been working, but with starving yourself and running like a mad man, I think you're losing weight too fast. It's not healthy, and I'm starting to worry."

"Don't." Nash kissed the top of Sidney's head. "I'm fine. Men just lose weight faster than women. Another month or two and I'll be back to the way I was when you first fell in love with me."

Sidney moved to straddle Nash's lap. "Is that why you're doing this? You think I need those washboard abs to find you sexy?"

Nash ran his hands down Sidney's flat stomach. "Don't lie. You used to love to touch my body."

"Yeah, and I still do. You fuckin' turn me on, ya bastard. Whether you have washboard abs or love handles, that's never going to change."

Despite the fact that he knew Sidney spoke the truth, Nash was still determined to restore his body to the way it had been. There were too many well-built men hanging around Sidney for Nash not to worry. It had all come to a head when Sidney's boss, Ben Shriver, had invited him and his entire family to the after-Thanksgiving brunch.

Nash had met Ben and his wife Abby on several occasions, but it was the first time he'd met Mike

Shriver, the man Sidney often worked close with on construction projects. Mike made Nash's mouth water and he wasn't even Nash's type. Still rock hard even in his mid-forties, Mike was not only gorgeous but funny. Even worse, he seemed to follow Sidney's every move with those dark green eyes of his. *Dammit!* Nash tried to push the jealousy out of his mind. He knew Sidney would never cheat, but how long could he resist a man who looked like Mike when he had to continue to come home to a man with a fucking beer belly?

"Pick a movie," Nash said, trying to get their evening back on course.

Sidney stared at Nash for several moments before climbing off his lap. He picked up three of the videos. "Hmmm, we've got garage workers, firemen or construction workers?" Sidney grinned. "You and your blue collar men."

Nash had purposely ordered the construction worker video as a sort of a test. Wrong or not, Nash needed to know if Sidney had fantasies about sex on the job.

"You have a preference?" Sidney asked.

"Nope. It's your birthday. Pick whichever one you want to watch first."

Movie in hand, Sidney stood and crossed to the VCR. He inserted the tape and turned around, letting the robe slip off his shoulders.

Nash's gaze flitted from Sidney's exposed body to the television screen. He wasn't aware he was holding his breath until the title of the movie flashed onscreen — *Climb my Pole*. Nash sighed. "Firemen, huh?"

Sidney shrugged. "They all look good, but the guy on the front of this one looks to have a really long hose."

* * * *

Spooned with his back against Nash's chest, Sidney whimpered when Nash's spent cock slipped from his hole. He was tempted to reach back and reinsert it but didn't want to wake his partner. Instead, he reached for the dildo Nash had used on him earlier and pushed it deep inside his stretched hole.

After an earlier nap while grease monkeys fucked each other's brains out on TV, Sidney was wide awake and ready for round three. He knew it was highly unlikely that either him or Nash could get it up again, but that didn't mean he couldn't enjoy the feel of having his ass filled while watching sweaty construction workers fuck and rim each other.

Sidney reached back and twisted the dildo, pushing it even deeper into his ass. Beside him, Nash let out a grunt, his peaceful sleep momentarily interrupted, before settling back into a soft snore. When the action on the screen got too hot for Sidney to sit still, he slid off the couch and pushed the coffee table out of the way. He found one of the toss pillows that had landed on the floor and stuck it under his head. Lying on his back, Sidney spread his legs and began to pump the dildo in and out of his body. It was nothing new for him to pleasure himself, so Sidney thought nothing of it.

"This tape got you so hot you have to resort to that?"

Sidney looked towards the couch to find a disapproving expression on Nash's face. "I didn't want to wake you."

Nash's gaze went from Sidney to the television. "Those construction workers are really doing it for you, aren't they?"

Normally, Sidney would readily agree and turn around to give Nash a show, but there was something in Nash's expression that stopped him. "What's going on?"

"You tell me."

Sidney removed the dildo and tossed it to the edge of the blanket that had fallen to the floor beside him. He sat up and turned to face Nash. "I wasn't quite finished for the night, but I didn't want to wake you. It's nothing new, so why're you all bent out of shape?"

Nash looked at the fucking construction workers once again. "You have fantasies about the guys you work with?"

"You mean do I think of having sex while at work? Who doesn't?" Sidney gestured towards the screen. "But that doesn't mean I have fantasies of fucking the men I work with. It's more the place than the people."

"What about Mike? You seem to talk about him a lot," Nash continued.

Sidney rose to his feet. He didn't know what the hell had got into his partner, but he refused to let Nash pick a fight with him on his birthday. The dreams he'd had involving Mike were no one's goddamn business. Never in a million years would Sidney act on them, so why should he be made to feel guilty about them? He hit the eject button and tore the tape from the machine. "Fucking burn it," he said, tossing the porn movie onto the couch beside Nash. "I'm going to bed."

"Did I hit too close to home for comfort?" Nash asked, stepping in front of Sidney.

"I don't know where this jealousy bullshit is coming from. I've never given you a reason to doubt my loyalty, never! Now get the fuck out of my way." Sidney tried to push past Nash, but Nash's strong arms wrapped around him, keeping him in place.

"I'm sorry," Nash said.

Sidney pushed against Nash's chest in an effort to get loose. He knew it was a combination of anger and guilt that fuelled his need to flee, but he didn't feel like listening to anything Nash had to say. It soon became obvious he wouldn't get away from Nash without starting an all-out fight between them. "Just let me go to bed," he pleaded.

Nash released Sidney and took a step back. "I'm sorry."

"Yeah, you already said that," Sidney replied on his way out of the room. He raced upstairs, deciding to jump in the shower before going to bed. As he stood under the spray, he tried to calm his pounding heart.

The dreams he'd had about Mike had constantly plagued him. It had started innocently enough with him making love with Nash, but at the moment of climax Nash had morphed into Mike Shriver. For two days afterwards, Sidney hadn't been able to look Mike in the eyes.

Sidney thought it was a one off, but a week later he'd had a similar dream. The guilt had been eating at him ever since. Did Nash have dreams about other men? In the past Sidney had pictured himself with celebrities buried deep inside him, but those were pure fantasy. The dreams about Mike were different and a lot more troublesome.

A shadow fell across him, and Sidney looked over to see Nash standing on the other side of the sliding shower door. Sidney held his breath. Had he cried out

Mike's name at some point in his sleep? Is that why Nash seemed so upset?

"You're right, I'm jealous," Nash admitted. "The shitty part about it is that I genuinely like the guy. I never really gave it any thought until I saw the two of you together at the Thanksgiving brunch."

Sidney tried to remember what he'd done at the brunch. "Did I do something to make you question me?"

"No, but I saw Mike following you with his eyes on more than one occasion that day."

Sidney turned off the water and opened the shower door. He'd noticed Mike's quiet interest in him, but Mike had never tried anything out of line. "I can't help the fact that Mike's attracted to me, but we both know where my heart lies."

"He's got a better body than I do," Nash mumbled, handing Sidney a towel.

"You can't compare yourself to him. Hell, Mike's got a better body than anyone I've ever seen, but you're the one I love. Do you honestly think I'd give up what I have with you to be another notch on Mike's bedpost? Come on, you know me better than that."

Nash nodded. "You're right. It's my problem not yours."

In all the years Sidney had known Nash never had he seen him so insecure. "I'd say it's *our* problem. Obviously I'm doing something to make you question yourself. Is it the weight thing? Because I've already told you it doesn't bother me."

"I know." Nash turned to leave the bathroom. "Forget it."

Sidney threw the towel on the floor and followed Nash into the bedroom. By the time he reached the bed, Nash was already under the covers facing away from Sidney's side of the bed. Although he'd been angry earlier, Sidney wanted nothing more than to comfort the man he loved. He spooned himself against Nash's back and rested his palm against the lightly furred chest he loved. "Do you love me less because of the scar on my face?"

"What? No. Why would you even ask me that?"

Sidney took a deep breath and ran his hand down Nash's chest to the slight swell of his stomach. "I feel the same about this."

"It's not the same," Nash mumbled, directing Sidney's hand away from his stomach.

"You're right it's not. You've got what, another ten or fifteen pounds to lose before you're back to the weight you were in your twenties? My face will never be the same, but I don't sit around and worry that you're going to jump into bed with someone else because of it. You know why?"

When Nash didn't answer him, Sidney continued. "Because I know that you love me. I've learned to accept the way I look because of you. What's it say about me that you're afraid I'd hop into bed with Mike because you've put on a few pounds over the years?"

With a heavy sigh, Nash turned over to face Sidney. "It's not just about the weight. I'm worried about a lot of things. I guess seeing the way Mike looked at you gave me something to focus all my frustrations on."

Sidney rested his hand on Nash's neck and brushed a soft earlobe with his thumb. "Let's forget about Mike. What else is bothering you?"

"We've got a lot of money tied up in the stock market. What if I fuck up and lose it all?"

Nash had been playing the market fulltime for several years, so why was he suddenly getting cold feet? "Why're you worried about it now? Did Peter say something when he was here?" Sidney asked.

Nash shook his head. "Peter had other things on his mind, like divorcing his wife."

The news shocked Sidney. "He told you that?"

"Yeah, but I don't want to talk about him." Nash grabbed the bottle of lube from the bedside table before pulling Sidney into his arms. "It's officially New Year's Eve, and I've yet to fuck you."

Sidney took the bottle from Nash and applied several drops to Nash's fingers. "Touch me," he whispered, directing Nash's hand to his ass.

Nash plunged two fingers deep into Sidney's hole. Sidney immediately moaned his appreciation for Nash's talented touch. "I could spend the rest of my life with your fingers right where they are," Sidney mumbled.

"That might get a little awkward when it comes time to leave the house."

"We could live on delivery and you could eat one handed." It sounded like a good plan to him. Sidney closed the distance between them and sealed his mouth over Nash's. As he explored Nash's mouth with his tongue, Sidney was reminded of all the reasons he loved him.

Sidney reached between them and greased Nash's cock without breaking the kiss. They'd been together for so long he didn't even need to ask for what he wanted next. Nash withdrew his fingers and held his cock by the base, waiting to give Sidney what was his. Their earlier argument could have escalated to a major blow-up if they were anyone but who they were, but it was to Nash's credit that he wasn't afraid to open himself like he had. Not only admitting that he worried about another man, but his fears about what the years were doing to his once toned body.

Sidney straddled Nash and lowered himself onto the thick erection that fit his him like it had been forged with his body in mind. "I love you," he whispered.

Nash's hands cupped Sidney's ass and spread his cheeks further apart, allowing Sidney to sink even lower on his cock. "You're my life. Without you I have nothing."

Sidney started to move, grinding his ass against Nash's groin. He stared down at Nash and fought an inner battle. The right thing to do would be to tell Nash about the dreams, but would the confession put Nash's mind at ease because he'd told the truth or would being honest only push Nash deeper into the depression he seemed to be battling lately? Sidney knew it was one of those times when he was damned if he did and damned if he didn't.

In the end, he decided to keep his dreams to himself. What purpose would telling the truth serve when he knew it would only hurt Nash? Besides, never in a million years would he cheat on the one man who'd always had his back.

"I feel the same way," Sidney replied.

* * * *

January 3, 1997

Sidney parked the rental car in front of the hospital and turned off the engine. "What the hell am I doing here?" he asked himself aloud.

He didn't need to think long. The phone call from his stepmother a few days earlier had prompted his change of heart. According to Sheila, Jackson was asking for Sidney. It was the first time in memory that Sidney had actually felt wanted by his father, but as he sat looking at the hospital, doubts began to creep into his mind.

How many times had he got his hopes up regarding his relationship with his father? Nope, he wouldn't do it. Jackson was a prick. He'd always be a prick and no amount of apologising would erase the things he'd done to Sidney over the years.

Sidney climbed out of the compact car and locked it before pocketing the keys. He entered the hospital and headed towards the bank of elevators, praying he wouldn't run into Sheila. He'd given her an approximate time for his arrival, so hopefully she'd cleared out for a few hours.

Pulling a slip of paper from his pocket, Sidney stared at the room number before making his way around the nurses' station towards his father's private room. According to Sheila, his father was living on borrowed time and she believed Jackson continued to hold on until he could set things right with Sidney.

Once he found the room, Sidney stood outside in the hall for several moments. He couldn't help but think he was making a mistake. It had been years since he'd seen his father and the pain the man had caused had scabbed and healed nicely, so why take a chance of reopening old wounds?

"Sidney?"

Sidney spun around and looked into the eyes of a woman not much smaller than he was, a pitcher of water in her hands. "Yes."

"I'm Sheila."

Sidney silently cursed his luck. "Hi."

Sheila's gaze went to the scar on Sidney's face. "Your father told me about your accident. I'm sorry."

Sidney shrugged. "It was a long time ago." Having a conversation with Sheila about the car accident that had sliced his face open and left one of his best friends paralysed served no purpose. He gestured to the open room. "Can I go in?"

Sheila handed him the pitcher. "If you'll fill his glass, I'll leave the two of you alone."

Sidney almost asked what she'd do if he declined. For some reason, he had the urge to tell the woman just what kind of father Jackson had been. Perhaps it was the need to hurt a man who couldn't fight back. Did that make him any better than a father who thought nothing of slapping his son to the ground for an innocent mistake? No. He took the pitcher and turned to enter the room.

A hand on his shoulder stopped him. "Please don't upset him," Sheila said.

Sidney couldn't believe what he'd just heard. "Excuse me?"

"I know the two of you haven't seen eye to eye in the past, but this is your chance to make up with him."

It was obvious Sheila knew nothing of Sidney's life with his father. Staring into her hazel eyes, it took every ounce of his control not to tell her exactly what kind of man she'd married. The only thing that stopped him was the realisation that Jackson must be a different kind of father to his new family. Did that make him feel better or worse? He had half-brothers/sister he'd never met, but was it their fault their sperm donor was an asshole?

"I appreciate what you're saying, but my relationship with my dad is my own. I won't go in there and start a fight, but I won't let him try to bully me either." Sidney turned away from Sheila, afraid of saying more.

Jackson's eyes were closed when Sidney entered the room. It gave him a chance to observe the changes in his father without being detected. The heavy-handed man he'd grown up knowing was nowhere to be seen. Instead, Jackson looked twenty years older than his fifty-three years. Oddly, a feeling of wellbeing filled Sidney. For the first time in his life, he didn't feel intimidated by this man.

Sidney walked to Jackson's bedside and refilled the glass on the table before setting the pitcher down. There were two chairs in the room, one beside Jackson and another in the corner of the room. Sidney opted for the one furthest away and sat on the edge.

A framed photograph on the window ledge caught Sidney's eye and he rose to examine it further. It depicted a happy-looking family with Jackson front and centre, surrounded by Sheila and three teenagers—a girl and two boys. For some reason the images of his half-brothers and sister threw him. Where he'd expected to see at least a little something of himself, there was none. The teenagers in the picture were all either blond or light brown headed. Did that have something to do with his dad being a nicer father to them?

"You came," a weak voice said from across the room.

Sidney set the photograph down and turned around. "Yeah."

Jackson stared at Sidney for several moments. "I figured you'd have had plastic surgery by now."

Sidney's hand went immediately to the scar. "I thought about it but Nash doesn't seem to mind it, and I was afraid of looking even worse afterwards."

"So Nash is still hanging around?"

"Yes."

"Figures. The boy's not stupid. He knows an easy meal ticket when he sees it."

"He's a day trader now. Truth be told, I think he probably makes more money than I do." Sidney squared his shoulders. "That's enough about Nash. Why did you want to see me?"

Jackson pressed a button that lifted the head of the bed into a more upright position. "I need you to do me a favour."

"You're kidding, right?"

Jackson's eyes narrowed. "No, I'm not. I could've caused a lot of problems for you when you got out of the hospital, but I didn't. I packed my shit and left the ranch like you asked. Now I need something in return."

Sidney shook his head. "You left the Running E because you were caught in your own web of lies. I'm the one who could have caused trouble for you. At least get the damn story straight." Every time Sidney thought about the way his father had lied to him about who actually owned the ranch his blood pressure soared.

"My oldest son works at the feedlot, has since he was a teenager. The problem is, the lot's not pulling in enough profit to keep it open. I was hoping I could send JJ to the ranch for a job."

"I'm your oldest son," Sidney reminded his father.

"I realise that, but you know what I meant. JJ eats, thinks and dreams of ranch life. If you won't do it for me, do it because he's your blood."

Sidney wasn't opposed to helping the kid out, but if he decided to ask Tommy — the man who had leased the ranch — to give JJ a job, it would be because he wanted to do it, not because Jackson asked. He decided to test his father further. "Does JJ know I'm gay?"

"What? Why would you ask me something like that? You think I care to discuss your perversions with a twenty-two year old?"

"Let me get this straight. I hauled my ass all the way to Colorado for you to ask me to do a favour for your son who you haven't told about me because I'm a pervert?"

"Will you do it or not?" Jackson asked, his jaw set in the stubborn position Sidney remembered well.

"I'll think about it after you're dead," Sidney said on his way out the door.

Sheila was waiting for him in the hall. "You're leaving?"

Sidney stopped and dug his wallet out of his back pocket. He pulled out a business card and handed it to Sheila. "Have JJ call me." He glanced over his shoulder towards Jackson's room. "I won't be back."

Chapter Three

June 1997

Sidney set down the phone and turned back to the design in front of him. He swallowed around the lump in his throat and tried to concentrate on his newest project, a modern glass and wood-beamed home.

He wasn't sure how long he stared at the drawing before a folded paper triangle hit him in the ear, bringing him out of his daze. Sidney glanced up and narrowed his eyes at Bobbi. "Cute." He retrieved the paper triangle from the floor and held it between his drafting table and his forefinger and shot it back towards his friend and co-worker. "Don't make me regret suggesting you for a job."

Sidney ended the statement with a grin when the paper hit Bobbi in the nose, bouncing off her glasses. He was just teasing, of course. Bobbi had worked at Creative Solutions for a little over a year and had become a good fit for the laidback company.

"It looked like you were thinking too hard. Who was on the phone?" Bobbi asked.

"My father's wife. He died yesterday."

"Nice of her to finally call."

Sidney shrugged. "Doesn't matter." His throat constricted around the words. He took a deep breath and squeezed his eyes shut. "I think I'll call it a day."

"Will you go to Colorado?"

Sidney shook his head. He didn't have to put up a front with Bobbi, she knew all about his non-existent relationship with his father. "I may ask Ben if I can take the rest of the week off though. Maybe Nash'll take a trip with me down to the ranch." He couldn't explain it, but he had an overwhelming desire to revisit the memories that still continued to haunt him. It had also been too long since he'd sat at his mother's grave. Although his mom had been dead since he was a boy, Sidney still sought comfort from her when life became too much for him to handle on his own.

Bobbi gave him her best smile. "Let me know if you need anything."

"Thanks. I will."

* * * *

Before driving up the ranch road, Nash pulled to a stop beside the family cemetery. "Do you want to visit your mom's grave before we head to the ranch?"

"I'll come down later," Sidney answered.

Nash shook his head in confusion and pulled back onto the road. They'd planned to leave first thing that morning, but Sidney had woken him around midnight and insisted they get in the truck and start their journey to the Running E. For someone who seemed to be in such a hurry to see his mother's grave, Sidney didn't seem overly interested.

Nash made a right and drove under the Running E sign. He slowed the truck and rolled down the window. His first inhalation of ranch air almost brought tears to his eyes. He'd never admitted to Sidney how much he missed ranch life. It was the reason he hadn't been back since the day they'd loaded the moving truck and headed to Chicago. "Can you believe it's been damn near seven years since we've been back?"

"Doesn't seem like it's been that long to me," Sidney said, turning up the air conditioner.

It seemed twice as long to Nash, but he didn't say it. "Feel like going for a ride this evening?"

Sidney continued to stare out the passenger window. "We'll see. You think Rosie will still remember you?"

Mention of his horse tore at Nash's emotions. "I hope so." He had no doubt Sidney was thinking about Diablo and Buckwheat and wishing they were still alive and on the ranch. Reaching across the seat, Nash brushed the side of Sidney's cheek with the back of his hand. His partner seemed so distant. "You okay?"

Sidney leaned into Nash's touch. "Not really, but I don't plan on leaving here until I am."

He's come home to heal, Nash thought silently. "Brynn said she'd run to the store for us this morning and get some groceries to stock the little house."

"That's good. I don't think I could deal with their bullshit right now."

Nash understood why Sidney felt that way. The townspeople had never welcomed him. "You ready for this?" he asked, gesturing towards the house. Except for the short time before they had left for

Chicago, Sidney was used to having the run of his family home. Would it seem strange to see another family in the house his grandfather had built?

"Yeah. I'm ready."

Nash stepped on the gas. For his part he had no reservations about returning to the Running E. Despite the fact that he wasn't raised on the ranch, it had always felt like home. The ranch had been Nash's entire world for too many years not to feel that way.

Sidney visibly tensed when Nash parked in front of the barn. "Mind if I take a walk on my own?"

"No. Do what you need to do. I'll be around when you're ready to head to the little house." Nash watched as Sidney got out of the truck and walked towards the chicken coop. *Fuck.* Suddenly everything became clearer. Sidney hadn't come back to the ranch to heal, he'd come back to remember. The chicken coop was the site of one of Jackson's worst beatings. Sidney had always hated that damn coop. It was the only explanation as to why he would seek it out first.

Movement from the house caught Nash's attention. He waved to Tommy before giving Sidney one last look. He hoped Sidney would find whatever it was he needed to deal with Jackson's death.

* * * *

Although the coop had been well cared for, it was haunting in Sidney's eyes. "I should've torn it down when I had the chance," he whispered.

He'd been barely five the first time his father had spanked him for shying away from gathering eggs. The chore didn't get any easier with age. How many times had he been told to be a man about it? God, he hated that damn phrase.

Before his mother's death, she would sneak out and gather the eggs for Sidney, but after she was gone it fell upon Sidney to face the coop daily. Sidney unconsciously moved his jaw back and forth, remembering the first time his father had actually punched him in the face. He couldn't have been more than twelve? Maybe thirteen? Sidney had made the mistake of shrieking when he'd almost grabbed a hidden snake in one of the nesting boxes.

If only Nash had been there that stupid Sunday morning. Jackson had rarely laid a hand on Sidney when there were witnesses around. After Jackson's fist had connected with Sidney's jaw, he'd pulled his son to his feet and made him reach back into the box and lift the large rat snake out with his bare hands.

When the snake decided to put up a fight, Sidney had made an even bigger mistake by pissing his pants in fear. Jackson had grabbed Sidney by his hair and marched him into the house. He'd made Sidney strip out of his clothes before leaving the room. Afraid and unsure of his father's plans, Sidney had allowed a single tear to drip down his cheek.

Jackson came back into the room carrying a hand towel and two safety pins. Despite Sidney's pleas that it would never happen again, his father fashioned the towel into a diaper and made Sidney wear it for the rest of the day. Although the episode had made a lasting impression on him, Sidney doubted it had been the lesson Jackson had hoped for.

Turning away from the coop, Sidney headed towards the barn where more memories awaited. He doubted there was a single structure on the ranch that had been left ghost free. Jackson's cruelty had long since overshadowed any good memories he'd had of life on the ranch with his mother and grandfather.

Although Nash loved the place, Sidney would have sold it long ago if it had been possible. Unfortunately, his grandfather's will prohibited it.

Nash's laughter reached Sidney before he made it through the barn door. He stopped and let the sound wash over him like an invisible caress. His earlier thoughts of selling the ranch vanished at the hearty laughter. The Running E was deeply entrenched in Nash's soul, something Sidney never understood but was grateful for. What would he have done all those years without Nash and his love for the ranch?

Sidney thought of the message he'd received on his phone from JJ. Although Sidney hated to admit it, ranch life seemed to call to JJ the way it had Nash. With summer upon them, Tommy would be looking to hire a few hands to help around the place. Why not do the right thing and suggest JJ?

Before Sidney made it farther into the barn, a hand clamped down on his shoulder. Sidney jumped and spun around. "You scared the crap out of me!"

Steve, a long-time ranch hand, chuckled. "Just like old times. You were always as skittish as a newborn calf."

Sidney had had good reason to be jumpy in his younger days, but he didn't say that to Steve. "That's because you've always thought it was funny to sneak up on me." Sidney grinned and held out his hand. "It's good to see you."

"You've grown," Steve replied, shaking Sidney's hand.

Sidney snorted. "Not an inch, but thanks for trying." He gestured towards the house. "How're things around here?"

"Good. Tommy's turned into a damn fine manager." Steve leaned closer. "He ain't so much for working the ranch anymore though, but don't tell him I said that."

Sidney decided it was a good time to bring up the subject of JJ. "Do you think he could use another hand?"

"Got someone in mind?"

Sidney nodded.

Steve lifted his Stetson and ran a hand through his thinning hair before settling the hat back on his head. "Sure wouldn't hurt, I can tell you that, but I'm not sure if the money's there right now."

Sidney nodded again. He wasn't sure how much JJ would need, but maybe Tommy could work out a deal with him. "I'll get with Tommy about it."

"Get with me about what?" Tommy asked, walking up with Nash at his side.

Sidney exchanged glances with Nash. Although he'd told Nash about the conversation he'd had with his dad months earlier, he hadn't told him he'd been thinking about JJ. "My half-brother needs a job. From what I hear he's a hell of a cowboy."

Tommy's eyebrows rose in surprise. "Jackson's other boy?"

"Yeah. The feedlot's about to close and JJ expressed an interest to work on the Running E. Would you give it some thought for me?" Sidney didn't want to put Tommy on the spot in front of Steve. He knew it would be a decision Tommy would probably talk over with his wife, Brynn.

"Sure," Tommy answered. "We can talk about it at supper tonight if you care to come over and enjoy some of Brynn's famous fried chicken."

Sidney glanced towards the coop. "Not a fresh one, I hope."

Tommy chuckled. "Hell no. Little Jake's named all the damn chickens."

Nash slapped Tommy on the back. "You mean you didn't teach him the number one rule of ranching?"

Tommy put his hands on his hips and shook his head. "Yeah, I told him, but once I saw him out here talking to them by name, I gave up. It's Brynn's fault for refusing to give Jake a little brother."

Sidney hadn't seen Jake since he was an infant. With the rest of Tommy's children near grown, Jake must get lonely on the ranch without any other kids. Sidney knew exactly what that felt like. Too bad Jake didn't have someone like Nash to follow around on the really boring days.

"Supper sounds good," Nash said.

"We even promise to shower first," Sidney added. He wasn't sure how he'd react to being in his old home again, but the entire point of coming to the ranch was to exorcise his demons.

* * * *

"Nash?" Sidney called.

"Yeah?"

"You wanna come in here and take a shower with me?"

Pausing in the act of doing his stomach crunches, Nash thought fast. "I'm in the middle of my exercises, but if you're still in there when I'm done I'll join you." He hated to lie to Sidney, but since New Year's Eve, Nash had been feeling even worse about his body. Was it a gay thing? He wondered how many other men hated their bodies. He was still angry that he'd let himself get to this stage.

Nash lifted his white undershirt and looked down at his stomach. Although he'd done a good job of losing most of his spare tire, there was no sign of the six-pack he used to have. He wanted to be the man he once was. A man who could proudly stand naked in front of Sidney and not worry that his partner's gaze was full of scrutiny.

Nash dropped his shirt and stood. He went to his suitcase and found the bottle of supplements he'd hidden amongst his underwear. With the weight finally coming off, Nash had begun work on his muscle development. He knew it was cheating, but Nash was bound and determined to regain the body he'd once had.

After swallowing the large pill, Nash finished his crunches. With each lift of his torso, he imagined himself standing bare chested beside Mike. The image powered him through the exhaustion he soon felt. By the time Sidney walked into the room dressed in nothing but a towel, Nash was still going strong. "You done?"

"Yeah. Why aren't you?" Sidney asked. He removed the towel from his waist and started soaking up water from his shoulder-length hair.

Nash rose to a sitting position and crossed his legs. "Guess I was just into it."

"Well you'd better get in the shower or we'll be late for dinner." Sidney crossed to the suitcase and pulled out a pair of cargo shorts and a T-shirt.

"I thought we were going riding after dinner?" Nash had looked forward to the evening ride all day.

Sidney stared at the shorts clutched in his hand. It was obvious to Nash that Sidney didn't want to go for a ride, but Nash hoped he'd go with him anyway. "Please?" Nash added.

Sidney dropped the shorts and retrieved a pair of blue jeans. "I didn't bring boots, so sneakers will have to be good enough."

Nash wanted to ask his partner why the hell he'd come to the ranch without his boots but decided to let it drop. "I'll just be a minute," he said, getting to his feet. He grabbed a clean shirt, jeans and underwear before going into the bathroom.

Closing the door, Nash heard Sidney make a snarky comment about his sudden modesty, but pretended he hadn't heard it. Sidney had made it clear a few months earlier that he didn't care what Nash's body looked like, but Nash wasn't buying it. Until he felt confident in his appearance, he'd continue to undress and change behind a closed door.

* * * *

Sidney squirmed in the saddle. It had been too long since he'd ridden a horse and his tailbone was protesting the constant motion. He glanced over at Nash. With his hat and boots on, Nash looked like a cover model for a western wear company. He'd somehow managed to slide right back into ranch life like he'd finally come home again. "Were these saddles always this hard?"

Nash chuckled. "Yeah, you're just getting soft in your old age."

A fun retort was on the tip of Sidney's tongue but he managed to swallow it before it left his mouth. He hated that he had to monitor himself lately. It was always a tossup as to whether or not he was supposed to mention Nash's weight-loss. The few times he'd tried to tell Nash he liked him no matter what, Nash didn't take the statement as intended.

Nope, better to just keep his mouth shut. Whatever was going on with Nash and his morphed sense of body image would hopefully work its way out of his system soon. "I don't suppose I could get you to go skinny dipping with me?" He dug into his pocket and pulled out a small bottle of lube. "I came prepared," he added, hoping to sway Nash to his way of thinking.

Nash looked towards the setting sun. "It'll be dark soon."

"All the more reason. Don't you want to make love in the moonlight?" *Please say yes.*

"With you? Always," Nash said, flashing a sexy grin.

Sidney practically swooned in the saddle. "God I've missed that."

"What?"

"You, looking at me like you really want me." Sidney bit his lip, afraid he'd said too much.

Nash drew Rosie up beside Sidney's horse. "I'll always want you." Nash leaned over and gave Sidney a quick kiss before pulling back.

They rode towards the creek that fed into the pond. They'd always preferred to swim in a particularly deep spot of the creek because the water temperature was always cooler than that of the pond.

When they arrived, Nash let out a low whistle. "Looks like we're not the only ones who enjoy this spot."

Once upon a time, tall weeds and grass had grown beside the creek. Now the entire area was nicely mowed with a bit of sand down by the water. A picnic table sat nearby, under a big cottonwood with a few small sand buckets and shovels on top.

There was something about the scene that caused an ache in Sidney's chest. "Looks like Tommy and Brynn must bring Jake down here."

"Yeah, I reckon." Nash got off his horse.

"It's nice," Sidney whispered, more to himself than Nash. What would it have been like to have a dad who cared enough to go swimming with him, let alone build him a private beach?

"Sidney?"

Sidney glanced down at Nash and smiled. "Sorry. Lost in my head."

"Well how about getting lost in my arms instead?"

Sidney slid off Jackpot's back and into Nash's embrace. When Nash started to release him, Sidney held on. There was something about the ranch that seemed to magnify his insecurities. The trip had already been a good reminder of how much he'd always relied on Nash for comfort. "Thank you."

Nash's arms tightened. "For what?" He brushed his cheek against the top of Sidney's head before following it up with a kiss.

"Everything." Sidney's eyes started to burn as he thought about the lonely boy who'd lost his mom. "I can't imagine what my life would've been like without you."

Nash tipped Sidney's head back and bent to give him a kiss. Sidney opened immediately, needing the intimate contact. As the kiss deepened, Sidney pressed his hand against the front of Nash's jeans. He outlined the growing cock through the worn denim and gave it a squeeze.

Nash insinuated his thigh between Sidney's legs and applied just the right amount of pressure to Sidney's erection. Oh, fuck. Sidney's hands began to shake as he worked to get Nash's fly open. "Need it," he groaned, breaking the kiss.

"Yeah," Nash agreed, pulling Sidney down on the freshly cut grass.

Nash's boots were soon tossed to the side as they both stripped out of their clothes. Naked, Sidney stretched out under the darkening sky and set the lube beside his hip. "It's been a long time since we've made love outside."

"Too long." Nash knelt and spread Sidney's thighs apart. He picked up the lube and applied a good amount to his hands.

Sidney moaned in anticipation of what was coming. Nash ran his hands across Sidney's chest. For several years after the car wreck, Nash had massaged Sidney's puckered scars on a regular basis, but he hadn't done it in a while. Slowly, Nash worked his hands over each scar, stopping to pay extra attention to Sidney's nipples.

Nash leaned over and took one of Sidney's nipples between his teeth. Applying the perfect amount of pressure, Nash slowly bit down.

Sidney released a ragged moan as the small bite sent erotic tingles throughout his body. "Yesss," he cried, pulling at Nash's short hair.

Nash groaned and made his way down Sidney's chest, alternating between sucking and biting the naturally bronzed skin. "Harder," Sidney begged when Nash reached his hip bone. It wasn't that he enjoyed the bruises that would follow such a request, but there were times when the right kind of pain helped him forget the suffering of his childhood. No doubt there were people out there who thought it was a twisted concept, but Nash had always understood him better than anyone.

Nash's first real bite landed on the tender flesh to the right of Sidney's cock. Sidney fisted his hands as Nash's teeth sank deep and hard. "That's it. Oh, fuck, that feels good."

Nash released the tortured skin and gazed down at the impression he'd made. "I nearly drew blood that time."

"Don't care. Loved it." Sidney slid out from under Nash and positioned himself on his forearms and knees. "Bite my ass," he begged.

Nash grabbed the bottle of lube once again and dripped several drops onto his fingers. He swiped at Sidney's hole several times with the flat of his tongue before inserting the tip of his forefinger. "Make your ass suck on my finger," Nash instructed.

Sidney's muscles clenched and unclenched around Nash's finger for several moments before he was rewarded with Nash's teeth on the cheek of his ass. The harder Nash bit, the more turned on Sidney became. "More in my ass," he panted.

Nash applied more lube to Sidney's hole before ending the erotic bite. "Want my cock, babe?"

"Yes. Need it. Need you."

When the tip of Nash's fat cock pushed against Sidney's hole, Sidney bit down on his own forearm in an effort to continue the high he was currently experiencing. "Slam it."

Nash pushed in to the hilt in one hard thrust. Although Sidney's ass was well used to Nash's cock, the sudden flash of pain nearly brought tears to Sidney's eyes. "Hard," Sidney mumbled.

Nash withdrew his cock and rammed it deep. "That hard enough?"

Unable to answer, Sidney nodded and bit harder into his own flesh. With each thrust of Nash's hips, a slap at the hand of his father was forgotten. He doubted even Nash could drive the demons completely from his soul, but he loved the man for trying.

A single tear fell from Sidney's eye as he shot his seed onto the grass below. He lifted his gaze to stare at the picnic table silhouetted in the moonlight.

"Shit!" Nash grabbed Sidney's arm and lifted it towards his face. "You're bleeding." He pulled Sidney to his feet and urged him towards the creek. "I know being here is hard on you, but I won't stand by and watch you hurt yourself because of it."

Sidney glanced down at his forearm. Twelve tiny wounds oozed blood. "It doesn't hurt."

"It will tomorrow." Nash held Sidney's hand as they waded into the cool water. "Was it necessary? Is my dick not enough to make you come?"

Sidney lifted his hands out of the water to frame Nash's face. "It's not you. It's this place." He stopped and shook his head. "Everywhere I look I'm reminded of how much I hated him."

Nash grabbed Sidney by the shoulders and shook him. "I'm sorry you had Jackson for a father, but you're thirty-three-years-old. It's time you put those memories behind you."

"I know. That's why I came here," Sidney whispered.

Nash moved to wrap Sidney in his arms. "When I look around the ranch, I see you, not Jackson. I see the little boy who followed me around while I did my work and the gangly teenager who used to wheeze and complain every afternoon when he did his chores." Nash pointed towards the bank. "And I remember making love to you right there once you'd healed after the accident. Those are the memories I took with me to Chicago. Jackson doesn't get them. They're mine."

Sidney gazed up at Nash. As usual his partner was right. He was allowing Jackson to ruin everything good he'd found living on the ranch. He wrapped his arms around Nash's neck and his legs around his lover's waist. "Just hold me."

Nash buried his face against Sidney's neck and began to turn around in a slow circle, dancing under the clear night sky. "Nash?"

"Mmm?"

"How come you don't talk about your dad?" Sidney asked.

Nash shrugged. "Never thought it was fair to you to bring him up, I guess."

"Why?"

"Because he was everything you deserved in a father but didn't get. Because he was my hero, and because the day he was killed was the day I started to drift away from my mother," Nash explained.

"You should visit her more," Sidney told Nash.

"Why would I do that when she makes you feel like shit every time we've been down there?"

"She's your mom. She doesn't have to like me for you to still have a relationship with her." Sidney nipped Nash's earlobe. "Promise you'll call her?"

"I'll think about it."

"Just don't think about it too long." Sidney thought of his own mother. She'd managed to save him by giving Nash use of the little house after her death. How had she known Sidney would need a man like Nash in his life?

Chapter Four

Sidney hung up the phone and went in search of Nash. He wasn't sure what he felt guiltier about, cutting his trip short or being happy about it. Dressed in cargo shorts and flip flops, he walked outside to Nash's pickup.

He drove the short distance to the ranch and parked in front of the barn. He spotted Tommy almost immediately. "Nash around?"

Tommy chuckled. "He's in the equipment shed working on the bailer. Any word from JJ on when he'll be here?"

"Day after tomorrow," Sidney answered. It was yet another reason he was happy about leaving. "I just got a call from work. A problem's come up that they need me to deal with."

"That's too bad. I think Nash was looking forward to cutting some hay before he left. It's supposed to be sunny on Thursday. I thought we'd wait and do it then."

As much as Sidney wanted to get back to his life, he knew how much Nash was enjoying himself on the ranch. It wasn't like Nash had a nine to five he had to get back to. Sidney didn't like the thought of going home by himself, but he hated to deprive Nash of sweating in the hot June heat. He'd never understood why Nash loved hay season. It was the worst time of the year in Sidney's opinion.

"I'll talk to Nash. Maybe he can drive me to the airport and stay a while."

"I'd appreciate it," Tommy said. "You know every pair of hands helps this time of year."

"Yeah, I remember." Sidney strode towards the equipment shed. By the time he reached his destination, his feet were covered in a fine, powdery brown dust. Nash was bent over with his upper body concealed by the large bailer. Sidney took a moment to enjoy the ass encased in an old pair of Wranglers. "Your ass is looking good," he said, announcing his presence.

Nash gave his ass a little wiggle before removing himself from inside the bailer. He turned towards Sidney and shook his head. "Flip flops? Really?"

Sidney shrugged. "When I dressed today I didn't know I'd have to tromp all over the ranch to find you." He walked over and gave Nash's ass a squeeze. "I wasn't kidding before. Your ass is killing me today."

Nash seemed pleased by the comment. "The exercises must be working."

"I'll say." Sidney ran his hands over Nash's rock hard ass cheeks. "Almost makes me wanna fuck you."

Nash's eyebrows shot up in surprise. Sidney had only topped a few times and it hadn't been anything to write home about for either of them. "We might just have to talk about that some more when I get done here."

Sidney didn't want to get Nash's hopes up, especially with the news he was about to break to his partner. "Ben called."

"Uh oh."

"Yeah. Evelyn Barnes has changed her mind again, and they're due to pour the foundation next week. Ben needs me back at the office to revise the blueprints."

"Can't he or Bobbi do it? Surely you're not the only one in the office who knows how to revise a drawing?"

"They have their own projects to work on. Besides, Evelyn likes me for some unknown reason and refuses to work with anyone else." The older woman had a sort of crush on Sidney that he couldn't explain. He'd been forced to tell the socialite he was gay and had a long-standing relationship. Neither had thwarted Mrs Barnes, who seemed dead-set on cheating on her husband with a younger man.

Before Nash had a chance to say anything more, Sidney decided to lay out his idea. "Why don't I fly back and you can come home after you've put up enough hay to satisfy the farmer in yourself?"

"You wouldn't mind?"

"Not at all. I'm not completely unaware of how much you've missed the ranch. I know you moved to Chicago for me, so do this for yourself."

"What about JJ? Aren't you the least bit curious about him?" Nash asked.

"Not really. I've seen his picture, so I know why my father favoured him. If I were to meet him, I'm afraid I'd spend the entire time comparing myself to him." Upon his return from his father's hospital bed, Sidney had told Nash about the tall, muscled blond man's picture at his dad's bedside.

"JJ may be a very nice guy," Nash argued.

"That's what I'm afraid of. I don't need another reason why there weren't any pictures of me in that room."

Nash shook his head. "You're being ridiculous."

The statement hurt. Whether or not he was right in his feelings towards his half-brother, it would've been nice to have Nash's understanding. "Maybe so, but that's the way I feel." Sidney stepped out of Nash's embrace. "I'm gonna go pack and call the airline."

"I'll be home in an hour or so," Nash said.

It was on the tip of Sidney's tongue to remind Nash that the little house wasn't his home anymore, but he swallowed the reply. Nash loved everything about the ranch and it was only his love for Sidney that had taken him away from it in the first place. Sidney needed to remind himself more often of Nash's sacrifices in the name of love. "Okay."

Sidney walked out of the shed. The trip to the ranch hadn't accomplished what he'd hoped. He'd wished to feel better about the decisions he'd made, but the visit only served as a reminder that his entire life hinged on Nash loving him. Where would he be if he lost that?

* * * *

Alone in the big backseat of Butch's ridiculous sedan, Sidney regarded his friends in the front. "You know this car doesn't suit you, right?"

Butch met Sidney's gaze in the rear view mirror. "SUVs are too hard for Luke to get in and out of."

In a sour mood, Sidney didn't bother to censor himself. "So what happens when you realise you've been driving around in a car meant for a senior citizen just to make Luke happy? Will you start to resent him and that damned wheelchair?"

"Sidney!" Luke admonished.

Without answering, Butch pulled into the nearest parking lot and turned off the ignition. He turned to level a steely gaze at Sidney. "What's your problem?"

Sidney buckled under Butch's stare. "Nothing. Sorry."

Butch shook his head. "Not good enough. You've been quiet since we picked you up at the airport. Are you mad because Nash stayed in Kansas?"

"No." Sidney knew explaining himself would only make him sound like an ungrateful child. "I said I was sorry. Will you just take me home, please?"

Luke repositioned himself so he could make eye contact with Sidney. "Are you going into work as soon as you get home?"

Sidney shook his head. "I told Ben I'd be there first thing in the morning."

"Then why don't we stop at the store and pick up some steaks to grill for dinner?" Luke asked.

Sidney glanced at Butch. Although he liked the big guy, Butch was first and foremost Nash's best friend. Not that he wanted to talk bad about Nash, but Sidney would prefer an evening where he could speak openly of his feelings without the threat of his words getting back to Nash.

Luke reached over and put a hand on Butch's shoulder. "Would you mind if Sidney and I spent the evening together?"

Sidney smiled at his friend. It was obvious Luke had picked up on Sidney's misgivings.

"Are you giving me permission to head to Wally's for the evening?" Butch asked with a wink.

Luke looked at Sidney. "Would you mind if we stayed in the downstairs guestroom tonight? I'd feel better if Butch could take a cab home from the bar."

"Not at all." Sidney found himself looking forward to an evening spent alone with his old friend.

"Promise me you'll take a cab to Sidney's?" Luke asked, rubbing Butch's earlobe between his fingers.

"Sure, if it'll make you happy," Butch replied.

Sidney rolled his eyes. As much as he loved and adored Nash, Sidney doubted he'd ever been as sappy as Butch was with Luke. He was happy that Luke had found such a great guy, but Luke's situation was much like Sidney's and that worried him. How would either of them survive without their partners at their sides?

* * * *

Sidney handed Luke another beer before resuming his position on the lounger. It was a beautiful evening, and as Sidney looked up at the stars, he couldn't help but wonder if Nash was outside enjoying the night sky as well. "Do you ever worry about what your life would be like if Butch left?"

"Not really, but thanks for putting it in my head," Luke answered. He was stretched out on a matching lounger, looking more comfortable than Sidney had seen him in a while. Butch had helped Luke onto the chair, and unfortunately, Luke would probably be there until Butch returned after his evening at Wally's.

"Is that what's going on with you right now? Are you afraid Nash's going to leave you? Because I'm here to tell you the man worships the ground you walk on."

"Don't get crazy," Sidney said around a chuckle. "Nash loves me, and I may be good in bed, but I'm hardly skilled enough to be worshipped."

"Whatever." Luke shook his head. "So answer the first question. Are you in this mood because you believe Nash will leave you?"

Sidney sighed. "Not really. I guess I just realised that everything I have, I have because of him. It worries me."

"That's bullshit." Luke took a drink of his beer. "I'm not saying Nash didn't help you along the way, but you're more than just Nash's partner."

"No." Sidney shook his head vehemently. "That's exactly what I am and I'm okay with it because that's all I've ever wanted. But in giving me everything, Nash gave up too much. He gave up the memories of his father because he was afraid of hurting me, he gave up his mom because she doesn't like me and he gave up the ranch because he knew I wasn't happy there. Someday he'll see that, and start to resent me for it."

"So what're you saying? Are you thinking about moving back to the ranch?"

"God no. I'd shrivel up and die there. That's what I'm saying. Nash has given up everything for me, and the one thing I know would make him the happiest, I can't bring myself to do. What the hell kind of person does that make me?"

"Although you seem to be enjoying your time up there on the cross, I happen to think Nash has a pretty damn good life here. He's got good friends, a job he loves and you. I'm sure if he wasn't happy you'd know it. So take him off the martyr list and just enjoy what the two of you have."

Sidney couldn't help but laugh. Luke always had the ability to put him in his place. "I love you, but you're an asshole sometimes."

"Right back at ya," Luke replied before taking another drink of his beer.

* * * *

After a long cool shower, Nash pulled on a clean pair of jeans and a T-shirt before leaving the bathroom. It had been decided that JJ would take over occupancy of the little house while working at the ranch as part of his pay. The deal worked out well for both Tommy and JJ and since Nash and Sidney rarely visited, it wouldn't be a hardship on them.

However, for at least another few days, it meant Nash and JJ sharing living space. Nash grabbed a bottle of water out of the fridge and joined JJ in the living room. "Bathroom's free."

Shirt already off and laying at his feet, JJ took another drink of his beer. It had been hard for Nash to resist indulging in the large quantity taking up space in the refrigerator, but he knew it would only set his conditioning back if he drank.

"I bought some hamburger when I was in town this morning. I thought we could grill if you're up to it," JJ said.

"Sure. I'll get the charcoal started while you're in the shower." Nash rose and headed towards the back door. It was increasingly obvious that JJ wanted to talk about Sidney, something Nash just wasn't comfortable with. He'd given JJ the basics, though. Nash was surprised JJ didn't even know what Sidney did for a living or where his half-brother called home.

From what Nash could tell JJ knew nothing about Jackson's relationship with Sidney. *Nope, none of my business*, he said to himself as he dug the charcoal out of the shed. The last thing he needed was to ruin JJ's memories of his father. He'd seen first-hand what that kind of pain could do to a person.

After setting the charcoal ablaze, Nash sat in one of the peeling metal lawn chairs and stared at the dying flames. The screen door slamming shut surprised him. "That was fast."

JJ sat down beside Nash and opened a beer. "You don't drink, do you?"

"I drink, well, I used to, until my body went to shit. I've been working hard to get it back and beer, even the light stuff, isn't on the diet."

"I find it hard to believe that a beer is going to do you any harm. You've got an incredible body."

Nash's spine stiffened. He looked at JJ, his mind buzzing with questions. "Are you gay?"

"Yeah, I thought you knew," JJ answered.

"No, I didn't." Nash tapped his fingers against the arms of the chair. "Did Jackson know?"

"I reckon. We never openly talked about it, but I never tried to hide it. I figured that's why he told me I should try and find a job on Sidney's ranch."

"Wait a minute, let me get this straight. You knew Sidney was gay, but you didn't know anything else about him?" Nash found it very hard to believe Jackson would impart that bit of information about his first born and leave out the rest.

JJ shook his head. "Jackson didn't tell me about Sidney, my mom did."

"But you're relatively sure Jackson knew you were gay?"

"Yeah. Like I said, I never tried to hide it. I even dated someone at the feedlot for a while. Why?"

Nash couldn't imagine a worse predicament to be in than where he currently sat. "Because Jackson hated Sidney. We just assumed it was because Sidney was gay."

JJ ran a hand through his wet blond hair. "Sorry, man, I don't know what to tell you. My dad didn't talk about Sidney, but I got the impression it was because something bad had happened between them and they'd had a falling out."

Nash couldn't hold his tongue any longer. "Yeah, something happened. Jackson knocked Sidney around once too often. When we found out he'd been lying and stealing from his own son, we kicked him off the ranch."

JJ's face drained of colour. "What're you saying?"

"Shit!" Nash jumped to his feet and headed towards the house. It was the exact conversation he hadn't wanted to get into with the younger man. "Forget I said anything."

"Oh, no you don't," JJ spat, catching up to Nash as he entered the kitchen. "You can't just throw out something like that and walk away."

"It's not my place…" Nash began.

"Fuck that. Would you rather I call Sidney and ask him to explain it to me?"

Nash leaned against the counter and crossed his arms. "Jackson wasn't a good father after Sidney's mother died. He rarely gave Sidney the time of day and when he did it was usually by screaming insults or hitting him. There. You happy?"

"No." JJ shook his head. "I don't even recognise the man you're talking about."

"Yeah, that's pretty obvious. Just like it was obvious to Sidney when he went to the hospital and saw the picture of your family, a family that didn't include him. I think that's the main reason he left before you got here."

"Mom always told us Sidney wanted nothing to do with us and not to bring it up around Dad." JJ opened the fridge and retrieved another can of beer.

"Hand me one of those, would ya?" Nash asked.

JJ reached back into the fridge. "I need to talk to my mom about this."

"I doubt it'll do much good. She didn't even know about Sidney until well after you were born."

"I don't understand. Where was Sidney while all this was going on?"

"Here. He was a teenager by then so Jackson thought nothing of leaving him for weeks at a time. I was here in the little house, so it was me who made sure Sidney ate and did his homework." Nash shrugged. "Truth be told, I think Sidney was happier when Jackson was out of town."

"If you'll excuse me, I need to go find out what my mother knew."

"Are you sure that's wise? She just lost her husband," Nash reminded JJ.

"I won't bring up most of it, but I need to know if Dad ever told her why he cut Sidney out of his life."

"I hope she knows. Because I can tell you it will crush Sidney when he finds out his dad accepted you but rejected him."

"I don't want that. I mean, I don't know him, but it sounds like he's had a rough time of it. No wonder he didn't come to Dad's funeral."

Nash didn't know what to say. His heart broke for Sidney, but he knew it wouldn't be easy for JJ to question his mom so soon after Jackson's death. "I'll make dinner while you make your phone call."

"Thanks."

"Don't thank me. I have a feeling you're in for an eye opening conversation."

* * * *

After a late meeting on Monday night, Sidney was busy gathering his blueprints when Mike walked over.

"Feel like grabbing something to eat before you head home?"

Sidney glanced around, hoping Bobbi was still in the building. He'd been so caught up in his thoughts he hadn't noticed everyone leave. "Uhhh, that's okay. I'll probably just go home and eat a sandwich or something. Nash is supposed to call tonight."

"It's just dinner. Since Thanksgiving you barely speak to me. Did I do something to piss you off?" Mike asked.

Sidney thought carefully before answering. He had to work with Mike almost on a daily basis. It wouldn't be a good idea to put him in an uneasy position by telling him Nash was jealous.

"Just dinner. I promise," Mike added when Sidney didn't immediately answer.

Sidney bit his bottom lip. If he went he'd definitely have to tell Nash about it later. "Sure," he finally agreed.

"Have you ever been to La Cocina?" Mike asked.

"Yeah, it's one of my favourites." Sidney could eat Mexican food every day of the week and not tire of it. He finished gathering his papers and set them on his drafting table as Mike shut off the lights.

"I'll follow you," Sidney said on their way to the parking lot.

Mike stared at Sidney for several moments before nodding. "Okay."

On the way to the restaurant, Sidney's guilt began to get the better of him. He knew he wouldn't be able to eat unless he told Nash. He dug his phone out of his pocket.

"Hello?" Nash answered, a distracted quality to his voice.

"You busy?" Sidney asked.

"Just grilling some burgers."

When Nash didn't continue, it sent alarm bells off in Sidney's head. "What's wrong?"

"Nothing that I can talk about right now."

"Is JJ there?"

"Yeah."

Sidney wondered if the two men were starting to get on each other's nerves. "Listen, I know you can't really talk, but I need to tell you something."

"Okay."

"I just got out of a meeting and Mike asked me to grab a bite to eat with him. We're going to La Cocina. I know I probably should've said no, but I have to work with the guy and offending him would only make things harder."

"Is Bobbi going?" Nash asked.

"No, she had a date she was hot to get home for. It's just dinner." Sidney cleared his throat. "You can trust me."

"I know," Nash whispered. "I'm just missing you."

Sidney smiled. He parked the car beside Mike's and held up his finger, indicating he was on the phone. "I miss you, too. When're you coming home?"

"We should have everything in by Friday, so I should roll in sometime Saturday."

"You know you can leave before all the hay's out of the field." Sidney hated sleeping alone, but what he hated even more was the thought that Nash would rather be at the ranch sweating than home with him.

"I know, but I'm enjoying myself. It's been a long time since I've put in an honest day's work."

"You mean it's been a long time since you've worked and sweated your ass off for little to no money," Sidney corrected.

Nash laughed. "Yeah, you're probably right about that."

In front of the car, Mike leaned against the brick wall of the restaurant and crossed his arms. The action drew Sidney's attention to the powerful muscles straining against the thin, light blue T-shirt. "Will you still call me later?"

"Of course," Nash answered. "What time do you think you'll be home?"

"Two hours, tops. This time of night, the traffic shouldn't be too bad."

"Okay. Love you."

"Love you, too," Sidney replied, closing his eyes. He remained in that position for several heartbeats after Nash hung up. Once again he told himself there was nothing wrong with being attracted to another man as long as he didn't act on it.

He joined Mike moments later. "Sorry about that."

"No big deal. Nash, I presume?"

"Yeah. He's staying until Saturday morning."

Mike beat Sidney to the door and held it open for him. "After you."

Sidney held up two fingers to the hostess and waited for her to grab two menus. "This way," she said.

"A booth if you have one," Mike said to her over Sidney's shoulder.

Sidney swallowed his protest. The only booths in the small family restaurant were set in the back, away from the large tables.

Once seated across from Mike, Sidney picked up the menu and pretended he hadn't already memorised it. Evidently he hadn't fooled Mike. He eventually pulled the menu out of Sidney's hands.

"Okay, tell me what I've done to piss you off."

"You haven't done anything."

Their waiter placed chips and two small bowls of salsa on the table. "I'm Todd, I'll be your waiter this evening. Can I get you something from the bar?"

"Margarita," Sidney and Mike said in unison, making Sidney laugh.

"Coming right up," Todd said, leaving the table.

Sidney picked up the salt shaker and held it over the chips. "You mind?"

"Not at all." Mike leaned his forearms on the table and waited for Sidney to finish before reaching for a chip. "Can I be honest with you?"

"Sure." Sidney dunked his chip into the salsa and put the entire thing in his mouth.

"I'm attracted to you," Mike announced, staring at Sidney.

Sidney nodded. "That's what Nash said."

"And he's jealous, I take it?"

"Something like that." Sidney busied himself with another chip. Where the hell was that drink? "I told him he was crazy. That a guy like you could have anyone you wanted, but he told me he noticed the way you looked at me at the Thanksgiving brunch."

"Obviously I can't have anyone I want or you'd be warming *my* bed instead of Nash's."

Todd appeared with their drinks, giving Sidney a chance to digest Mike's statement. "Thanks."

"Have you decided on dinner?" Todd asked.

"I'll have the number three, no jalapeños," Sidney ordered.

"Shredded beef burrito and I'll take his jalapeños."

Sidney took a gulp of his frozen margarita, hoping the brain freeze would drive thoughts of Mike's bed from his mind.

"Does it make you uncomfortable to know I think about you all the time?" Mike asked.

"You know it does." Sidney decided to lay his cards on the table. "Look, Mike, I'm not about to lie and say I'm not attracted to you, but I have Nash."

"What if Nash weren't in the picture?"

A sense of calm suddenly came over Sidney. "If Nash weren't in the picture, I wouldn't even be here. Without Nash I'd either be dead or wasting my life somewhere else. He's the best part of me and the reason I am where I am today. I like working with you, but if this is going to be a problem, I'm sure there's another job out there I could get."

Mike smiled. "I won't say I'm not disappointed, but it's nice to see monogamy in action. I promise to never come onto you again." He winked. "Unless of course something happens between you and Nash."

"Nothing's gonna happen to tear us apart. I can guarantee you that much." Sidney felt one hundred per cent better. He couldn't wait for Nash to come home.

* * * *

The minute Nash set his suitcase down, Sidney jumped into his arms. "You're so tanned."

Nash hoisted Sidney higher and carried him to the sofa, settling Sidney on his lap. "JJ talked me into driving the tractor without a shirt on."

"How's JJ doing?" Sidney asked.

"Good, I think. He's having a rough time with everything he found out about Jackson, but he was doing better yesterday."

Sidney reached down and pulled Nash's T-shirt over his head and off. "When you first told me why Dad hated me so much, it hurt, but I've come to realise that I detest him even more knowing money was behind it all. I mean, how dare he take the provisions of my mother's will out on me. I was just a kid."

Nash was surprised Sidney was taking the new revelations so well. "I think that's what JJ's having the hardest time with as well." He ran his fingers through Sidney's silky black hair and pulled him in for a kiss. He lapped at Sidney's lips for several moments before thrusting his tongue deep into Sidney's warmth.

Sidney started to wiggle his ass against Nash's cock as the kiss became an all-out tongue fucking. Nash pushed his hands down the back of Sidney's sweatpants and grabbed the twin globes. He worked his way towards the centre of Sidney's heat and rimmed the puckered skin with the pad of his middle finger. "Damn, I missed you," he said, breaking the kiss. He withdrew his hand and licked his finger before touching Sidney's hole once again.

Sidney squirmed until Nash's fingertip pushed inside. "Aaahh," Sidney moaned.

"Have you been needing, babe?" Nash asked.

Sidney nodded. "Wore out a set of batteries waiting for you to get home."

Nash could attest to that fact. It seemed every night when Nash called to check in with Sidney, he found his lover with a dildo up his ass, begging Nash to talk dirty to him. Not that Nash minded. Hell, his right hand had become his best friend over the last week and a half. "Let's go upstairs."

Sidney gestured to the bottle of lube on the coffee table. "I brought stuff down here because I knew I wouldn't be able to wait."

Nash stood with Sidney still wrapped around him. "Grab the lube so I don't have to take my finger out of your ass."

With a chuckle, Sidney reached down and swooped up the bottle. "It's been years since you've carried me to bed."

Although he knew Sidney didn't mean it as a cutting remark, Nash internalised it that way. "I'm stronger now than I used to be." As he started up the steps, Sidney's free hand roamed his chest.

"I believe it. Your upper body is looking amazing."

Satisfied that Sidney noticed how hard he'd been working to get his body in shape, Nash took the last several steps two at a time. "Once I get you in bed, don't plan on getting out of it until Monday."

By the time Nash dumped Sidney on the king-sized mattress, his heart was pounding. It wasn't the fast rhythm that went with exercise but something different. Irregular was the word that came to mind. He pushed away thoughts of worry and told himself it was the desire he felt for the man in his arms and nothing more.

Nash watched Sidney strip off his sweatpants before he began to undress. Standing naked over Sidney, Nash grinned. "Prepare to be fucked for the next thirty-six hours."

Sidney glanced at the clock. "Actually, it's thirty-eight hours, but I guess I'll allow you two hours of rest between now and Monday morning."

Chapter Five

October 1997

Slumped over in a chair, Nash rubbed his chest, hoping to ease the tightening he felt. In front of him were the numbers, indicating his loss for the day. One day and much of the money he'd earned in the last year was gone. Why had he ever decided to gamble his money on the stock market?

Nash reached out and shut off the computer before slowly getting to his feet. If he could just make it to the bed, he was sure his breathing and heart rhythm would return to normal. It was just the shock of the crash that had caused the anxiety attack, nothing more.

Once he'd made it to the bedroom, Nash fell into bed and rolled to his side, curling his body inward. He stared at the phone and wondered if he should call Sidney. If it really was an anxiety attack, he'd feel like a fool for pulling Sidney off the job site, but what if it was something more?

Sidney was all the way down in Lincolnwood, working on his newest project. Not only would he be upset that Nash had called him home for something frivolous, but when he found out how much money Nash had lost in the market within a few hours, he'd be furious.

Closing his eyes, Nash tried to put thoughts of the stock market out of his mind as he concentrated on slowing his breathing. Dammit, he was in the best shape of his life, why was this happening to him?

He must've fallen asleep because the next thing he knew, Sidney was seated beside him, ruffling his hair. "Wake up, sleepyhead."

Nash smiled up at his partner. "What time is it?"

"Almost seven. I thought we were going out for dinner, but if you're too tired, I can probably find something to throw together."

Nash reached out and wrapped his arms around Sidney. "Just lay with me for a few minutes and then we'll leave."

Sidney kicked off his shoes and stretched out beside Nash. "I heard about the mini-crash on the way home from work. Was it bad?"

Nash rested his head against Sidney's chest and nodded. "Real bad." He took a deep breath. "I'm sorry."

"Why're you sorry? Did you cause it?"

"No, but I lost a lot of money."

"So, you'll pull back, regroup and charge forward again. Isn't it you who told me losing money is as much a part of the market as making it? The important thing is not to panic. We're not headed for the poorhouse anytime soon, so we'll ride it out if we need to."

Nash scooted up to share the pillow with Sidney. "I was so worried that you'd hate me."

"That's ridiculous. Even if we'd lost everything I couldn't hate you."

The longer Nash lay with Sidney the less he felt like getting up. The day's stress had really taken its toll. "Why don't we order a pizza or Chinese?"

"Okay. Of course you know one of us will have to eventually get up and answer the door."

"I nominate you," Nash mumbled, kissing the side of Sidney's neck.

* * * *

"Come on, we're going to be late," Sidney yelled just as the doorbell rang. He grabbed the bowl of miniature candy bars off the entry table and opened the door. Sidney jumped, pretending to be frightened of a six or seven-year-old vampire. "You scared me."

The small boy laughed, dislodging his plastic fangs. "Trick-or-treat."

Sidney dropped a few pieces of candy into the giant orange pumpkin head and smiled. "Have a good Halloween." He shut the door and started yelling for Nash once again. "Come on before these little goblins eat all my candy."

Nash finally came down the steps still buttoning his shirt. "Sorry. I was talking to Peter. He thinks Amazon's going to split their stocks in the near future, so I took a good look at my portfolio and decided to buy up as much as I could afford to lose."

Sidney rolled his eyes. It had only been a few days since the mini-crash and already Nash seemed obsessed with earning back the money he'd lost. "It's

Halloween. Can we please not talk about the market tonight?"

Nash paused in the process of putting on his black leather jacket. "Sure."

"Thank you." Sidney stood on his tiptoes and gave Nash a quick kiss. "Now let's get out of here before anyone else rings the bell."

"They'll egg our house if we're not here to give them candy," Nash reminded.

"I'll take my chances." He locked the front door and followed Nash to the garage. They didn't have anything big planned for the evening, just cards with Butch and Luke, but Sidney was looking forward to getting Nash out of the house for the first time in days.

As Nash pulled out of the garage, Sidney remembered the phone call he'd received earlier. "Oh, Butch wants you to stop by and get some more beer on the way."

Nash made a noise that sounded suspiciously like a growl. "Why does he always invite us over but make us buy the beer? Tight ass."

Sidney reached across the seat and put a hand on Nash's knee. "He invites us over because it's easier for Luke for us to meet at their house. What's with you all the sudden? You never seemed to mind stopping for beer before."

"Nothing. It'd just be nice if Butch would actually have it once in a while," Nash continued to grumble.

Sidney withdrew his hand before Nash had a chance to bite it off. He sure as hell hoped a night with friends would be enough to improve his partner's mood, because he'd had his fill of it.

* * * *

Halfway through the evening, Nash escaped to the seclusion of the small bathroom. He closed the toilet lid and sat down before resting his forearms on his knees. Although he loved Sidney with all his heart, he wasn't in the mood to listen to Luke and Sidney volley insults back and forth. Not right now. Not when he had so many other things on his mind.

What he'd passed off as an anxiety attack had evidently been something more because he'd had a similar episode in the shower earlier that evening. It had taken all his strength to dress and face Sidney without falling down the stairs.

He'd hidden his worry behind a mask of anger directed towards Butch for daring to ask for a fucking twelve pack. Nash stood and ran cold water in the sink before splashing his face. Maybe he was worrying over nothing. It was possible he was just having an adverse reaction to the new protein powder he'd started drinking.

"That has to be it," he told his reflection. He'd throw the damn stuff out the minute he got home. If his symptoms didn't improve in a couple of weeks he'd make an appointment with a doctor.

A knock sounded. "Are you okay?" Sidney asked.

"Yeah." Nash dried his face on a hand towel before opening the door. He smiled down at Sidney, feeling better now that he thought he'd figured out what was going on with his health. "Ready to play?"

Sidney shook his head. "You've been in here for over twenty minutes. Butch and Luke are ready to watch the movie now."

"Oh, okay." Nash followed Sidney into the den. Luke had already been helped onto the double-wide chaise with Butch lying next to him.

"Something you ate?" Butch asked around a chuckle.

"Shut up," Nash fired back. He took his customary position on the sofa and waited for Sidney to curl up beside him. "I brought the beer so you have to make the popcorn."

"Later."

Nash wrapped his arm around Sidney as Butch started the movie. He hoped it was one he'd already seen because there was no way he'd be able to concentrate enough to follow it.

Sidney rested his head on Nash's chest. "Sure you're okay?"

"I'm fine. Don't worry." He prayed those words were true.

* * * *

November 1997

"Sidney!" Nash yelled from the living room.

"I'm checking the turkey," Sidney yelled back. "I'll be there in a minute." He slid the large bird back into the oven, making sure the foil stayed over the roasting pan and shut the door.

For the hundredth time that morning, Sidney wondered why he continued to host Thanksgiving. He loved the concept of having everyone he cared about in one location, but rarely did he manage to get through the day without at least one breakdown.

To add to his stress level, JJ had called and asked if he could join them for the holiday weekend. Refusing the request didn't feel like an option, but Sidney wasn't ready to meet his half-brother with an entire house full of people watching.

After a quick wash of his hands, Sidney entered the living room. "What?" he asked with impatience.

Nash stopped mid-conversation and gestured towards the handsome man he'd been talking to. "JJ's here."

Crap. Sidney thrust himself forward, hand extended, knees threatening to buckle. "Nice to meet you."

JJ stood and grasped Sidney's hand, using it to pull him into a hug. "I've waited a long time for this, big brother."

Sidney swallowed around the lump in his throat. He wasn't sure he was ready to be a big brother to anyone. He'd felt like an only child his entire life. Was someone really family just because they shared half the same gene pool? His friends were his family and they didn't share a drop of blood between them.

Sidney looked at Nash, silently pleading for help when JJ didn't immediately release him. He gave the younger man a couple of friendly pats on the back, but he didn't feel comfortable hugging him just yet. It wasn't that he didn't sympathise with JJ, because he did. The man had learned the worst parts about their father in the months since Jackson's death, but for some reason the hug felt...forced.

"Why don't we get your luggage?" Nash suggested.

JJ squeezed Sidney once more before stepping back. Sidney was surprised to see tears in JJ's big blue eyes. "I'm sorry," JJ whispered for Sidney's ears only.

Something inside Sidney shifted as he looked into those watery eyes. "Not your fault," he returned, honestly feeling the words for the first time.

JJ's Adam's apple bobbed several times as he blinked away his tears before turning to Nash. "I just have the one bag, so I'll get it."

The moment JJ left the house Nash walked over and hugged him. "You okay?"

Instead of automatically saying he was fine, Sidney really thought about it. For whatever reason, JJ obviously wanted to have a relationship with him. Sidney didn't know why he hadn't heard from his other half-brothers and sister, so he had no idea what JJ's relationship was with them. What if JJ felt like an oddball in his own family and was searching for a place to belong? Could Sidney really turn someone like that away?

"Yeah," Sidney finally said. "The hug was a little uncomfortable, but JJ seemed to need it, and I'm okay with that."

JJ knocked on the door before opening it, bag in hand. "Are you sure you don't mind me staying here?"

"Not at all," Sidney replied. "As long as you don't mind sharing a room with Eric. Don't worry, there are two twin beds in the room."

JJ grinned. It was the first glimpse of the man's charm. "I don't mind sharing."

Nash cleared his throat. "Eric's a real ladies man, so you're probably out of luck there."

JJ shrugged. "Ya never know."

Nash laughed and gestured towards the downstairs guestroom. "Right through that door."

JJ nodded and carried his suitcase out of the room.

"Do you think he'd really hit on Eric? That could be a disaster." Sidney didn't want to make Eric uncomfortable, although Eric loved to make Sidney uneasy by talking about tits and pussy. "Scratch that. I wouldn't mind seeing Eric on the receiving end of JJ's obvious charm."

"You're evil," Nash said around a laugh.

Smiling, Sidney shrugged. "I'll be in the kitchen. Send Luke in when he gets here."

"Are you going to put him to work again? I had to hear about it all day last year."

"It's good for him. Butch babies him like his mother does."

Nash kissed Sidney's forehead. "No more than I baby you."

"That's a damn lie and you know it," Sidney countered.

"Is it?" Nash asked as he laughed and left the room.

Sidney narrowed his eyes and cussed Nash under his breath as he retreated back to the kitchen.

* * * *

The Ballentine family took over clean-up duty with Sidney's supervision. He'd been told to sit at the kitchen table and instruct where things went without lifting a finger. Watching the Ballentine boys try to get along well enough to put away the food and do the dishes was the best after dinner show Sidney had ever seen.

"I miss your parents," Sidney said. "I mean, I understand why they didn't come this year, but it feels weird not to see them."

Peter placed the stack of china plates in the glass-fronted cabinet. "They refuse to give up on Josh. So when he called and asked them to visit him in rehab for the holidays, they dropped everything."

It was Josh's fourth time in a rehab programme, and sadly, Sidney didn't hold out much hope that he'd stay clean for long. His feelings seemed to be echoed by the rest of the brothers, but no one except Luke had come right out and said it.

"So what's the deal with your brother?" Eric asked. "I didn't even know you had a brother."

"JJ's my half-brother. I met him for the first time this morning, although I've spoken to him on the phone a couple of times since my dad died." Sidney wasn't sure how much of his life the rest of the Ballentine family knew, so he decided to just give them the basics.

"So why isn't he in here helping us with the clean-up?" Eric asked.

"Because not only did he drive all night to get here, but he peeled the potatoes." Sidney narrowed his eyes at Luke who hadn't shown up until right before dinner.

"Hey, at least I called to tell you I had to go to the airport with Butch."

Sidney wasn't mad at Luke, but Luke didn't have to know that. "Yeah because Butch didn't know his way to the fucking airport," Sidney shot back.

"Whatever," Luke grumbled.

"And he's getting out of doing the dishes," Zac added.

"Not my fault I can't reach the sink," Luke defended himself.

"Bitch. Bitch. Bitch," Zac mocked his older brother.

Sidney smiled, knowing no one in the room took the ribbing personally. Bickering was as much a part of Thanksgiving as the turkey.

The kitchen door swung open and Butch walked into the room. "Am I gonna have to separate you kids?"

"No," several of the brothers said at the same time.

"They're picking on me," Luke told Butch.

Sidney waited for Butch to defend Luke, but Butch just grinned. "You love it, and you know it. Just keep it down so we can hear the game." Butch gave Luke a quick kiss before grabbing several bottles of beer out of the fridge. "By the time you guys stop messing around and get everything cleaned up, I'll be hungry again."

Peter threw a dishtowel at Butch's back as he headed out of the kitchen. Yep, a typical Thanksgiving.

* * * *

Sidney was the first one up the following morning. He didn't bother taking a shower, having taken one before bed. He dressed quietly and crept out of the room without waking Nash. Post-Thanksgiving brunch had been his idea, so he always tried to handle the details on his own. Besides, Nash had looked exhausted the previous evening.

At the bottom of the stairs, Sidney stopped in his tracks at the sounds coming from the downstairs guestroom. He stepped lightly as he neared the door. The noises were unmistakable. *Shit.* JJ was a fast worker, he'd give his brother props on that much. He listened for a few more minutes until the sounds started giving him a hard on. *Gross. That's my brother.*

Icked out by his reaction, Sidney left the two men to their passion and walked to the kitchen. He was surprised to find Peter sitting at the table drinking a cup of coffee. "What're you doing up?"

Peter glanced up from the morning paper. "My room is right above the downstairs guestroom. I don't think I got a wink of sleep all night."

"Did you know?" Sidney poured himself a cup of coffee and joined Peter at the table.

"About Eric?" Peter shrugged. "No, but it doesn't surprise me. His mind's been on nothing but sex since he was fifteen. But that doesn't mean I want to hear it. Hell, it's been almost a year since I've…" He shook his head. "Never mind."

"Sorry about Janet."

"Don't be. I knew long before she left that she'd fallen out of love with me. I tried, but it doesn't really work when it's all one sided."

"And there's been no one since?" Sidney knew he was prying, but it was rare for Peter to talk about anything other than business.

"No. I decided to take some time to get myself together. You know, get over the bitterness."

"And have you?"

"I think so." Peter rose and refilled his cup. "Is your friend going to be here today?"

"Bobbi? Yeah." Sidney remembered how well the two of them had got along last year. "Let me warn you though. Bobbi is not allowed to move to Philadelphia. Got it?"

Peter chuckled. "I was thinking about asking her to dinner, not to move in."

"Yeah, well, you say that now, but you haven't been around her as much as I have. Believe me, if I was straight, Bobbi would be it for me."

"I'll remember that."

"Good." Sidney slapped the table and stood. "How good are you at peeling potatoes?"

* * * *

Sidney cornered Eric in the kitchen before the rest of the guests arrived. "Anything you want to tell me?"

Eric crossed his arms. "Do you really want a *blow-by-blow* account of my night with your brother?"

"No. I was just surprised when I came down this morning and heard the two of you going at it."

"He's a fucking maniac in the sack."

"Yeah, well, that's a little too much information. What I didn't know was that you swung that way, or is JJ the first?"

"First, last, does it matter? I like him and that's good enough for me."

It was obvious he wouldn't get a straight answer from Eric, so Sidney changed the subject. "So no one wants to talk about it, but I need to know how Josh is really doing."

"Honestly? I don't really know. Mom and Dad seem to think he's hit rock bottom and has nowhere to go but up, but I'm not convinced."

"Do you think I should go see him?"

"No. I don't think any of us should see him until he proves to us he can stay clean."

"But maybe it would help him to know he has a support system," Sidney began.

"He's had a fucking support system his entire life and it hasn't changed a thing. He just keeps trying to drag everyone else down with him. He's my brother and I love him, but until he cares enough for himself and his family to stay clean, I'm done with him."

Sidney wasn't surprised at Eric's anger. Josh was the older of the two. It was just a shame the man hadn't really grown up.

JJ walked into the kitchen with a smile. "Hey," he greeted.

Eric didn't even flinch when JJ stopped in front of him and bestowed a deep kiss. In fact, Eric wrapped his arms around JJ and took the kiss to another level.

"I'll go check on the table set-up," Sidney said when the two men started grinding against each other.

He escaped to the garage where he found Nash and Peter talking business. "Everything all set out here?"

"Yeah, but we can't get another table or chair in here, so if you keep adding people, we're going to have to find a building to rent or something."

"Or we could buy a bigger house?" Sidney suggested. He'd always dreamed of designing and building his own home.

"In this economy? Are you crazy?" Peter piped in.

"Unless you're sleeping with me, you don't get a say," Sidney told Peter.

"He's right you know." Nash reached out and threaded his fingers through Sidney's. "Maybe someday."

"Yeah, someday," Sidney mumbled. He kissed the back of Nash's hand before pulling away. "I'd better go back so I can listen for the doorbell."

"Aren't Eric and JJ in there?" Nash asked.

Sidney exchanged a glance with Peter. "They're preoccupied at the moment. Maybe Peter can fill you in." He left Peter sputtering as he walked around to the front door instead of taking a chance on interrupting something in the kitchen.

Although he didn't mind Eric and JJ getting together, Sidney hoped it wouldn't make things awkward for the Thanksgivings yet to come.

Chapter Six

July 1998

"No, Lionel's decided he wants this whole wall made entirely of windows," Sidney said. "You're going to have to rip all this sheetrock out and redo it." Standing in the kitchen of his most recent project, Sidney went over plan changes with Mike. He hated it when customers made last minute changes, but at least they were told upfront this would incur an additional charge.

Mike wiped the sweat off his forehead. They were in the middle of an unusual heat wave and the air conditioning had yet to be fully installed. "Have the windows been ordered?"

"Yeah, but they won't be here until day after tomorrow."

Mike's cell phone rang, interrupting Sidney. "Hang on." Mike pulled the phone out of the holster on his belt. "Mike," he answered.

Sidney watched as Mike's dark eyebrows drew together. "We're on our way." He hung up the phone. "Your phone's off," he told Sidney.

Sidney dug the phone out of his pocket. "Shit. I turned it off this morning when I met with Lionel."

"That was Ben. The hospital called you and when they couldn't get through, they called work. Nash was brought into the emergency room a few minutes ago. He collapsed at the grocery store."

It took a moment for Mike's statement to sink in. "What?"

Mike began pulling Sidney towards the front of the house. "We need to get to the hospital."

Sidney yanked his arm out of Mike's grasp. "Wait a minute. I don't understand. Is he okay?"

"I don't know!" Mike yelled. "Let's just get you to the fucking hospital."

Sidney barely held himself together as Mike loaded him into his truck. The moment they were on the road headed towards Northwestern Lake Forest Hospital, Sidney gasped and struggled to breathe.

Mike reached over and shoved Sidney's head down. "Don't you go passing out on me."

"Is he dead and you're just not telling me?"

"I don't know anything more than what I told you."

"Call Ben. Ask him," Sidney pleaded. He was thirty minutes away from the hospital. A lot could happen in thirty minutes.

Sidney's mind raced with possible reasons for Nash's collapse. "Maybe he just fainted," he mumbled.

"Maybe."

Sidney concentrated on his breathing. He wouldn't be any help to Nash if he arrived at the hospital a hysterical lunatic. "I should probably call his mom."

"Where's she live?"

"Phoenix." Sidney wasn't even sure he had Loretta's current phone number.

"I'd wait until you get to the hospital and find out what's going on. No sense alarming her if it's nothing."

"Yeah, you're right." Sidney sat up and angled his body away from Mike. He had a strong feeling he could break into tears at any moment and didn't want to do it in front of the other man.

"Nash's been tired a lot lately, but I thought it was because he's been working so hard. I should've known something was wrong."

Mike's hand landed on Sidney's shoulder and gave it a comforting squeeze. "Don't. Just hang on until we get there."

"He's my life," Sidney said, his eyes filling with tears.

"I know."

* * * *

Sidney paced the waiting room in a foul temper. He'd been there for over fifteen minutes and still no one would give him definite answers to his questions. He'd learned that Nash had suffered a heart attack at the store and luckily the store manager had come to his aid almost immediately to start CPR. Nash had managed to survive the ambulance ride and was currently being attended to. That was it. "Where the hell's the doctor?"

"He'll be out as soon as Nash is stabilised," Ben reminded him.

Sidney glanced at his boss who was sitting between Mike and Bobbi. "I need to know he's going to be okay. Don't they understand that?" He knew he sounded irrational, but damn it, he needed answers.

Bobbi walked over and wrapped her arms around Sidney. "It's okay, sweetie. Nash's strong. He'll be okay."

Staring into Bobbi's eyes, it took every ounce of strength he possessed not to collapse to the floor. "I yelled at him this morning. We were out of milk and he was supposed to go shopping yesterday but didn't."

"It's a good thing he went to the store." Bobbi smoothed the hair out of Sidney's face. "He was with people who could help him, so maybe you should be grateful you yelled at him."

"He's just been so lazy lately. I was so angry I didn't even tell him I loved him before I left for work. I never do that." Sidney would never forgive himself if he'd lost the chance to say it again to the man who meant everything to him.

"Mr Wilks?" a deep voice said from behind Sidney. "I'm Dr James Colter."

Sidney turned to face an older man in scrubs. "How is he?"

"Stable." The doctor gestured to an area in the corner of the waiting room. "Let's go over there and talk."

Sidney gave Bobbi's hand a squeeze before releasing it. He followed the doctor to the corner grouping of chairs and sat. "Tell me."

"Mr Nash suffered a myocardial infarction, medical term for a heart attack."

"Yes, they told me. Do you know what caused it?"

"I've spoken to Mr Nash's cardiologist. We've concluded that the antiarrhythmic Mr Nash has been taking wasn't enough to control his arrhythmia. We're currently trying to determine the best treatment. We may be able to perform an electrical cardioversion, which basically means we try to reset the heart's rhythm. It's often an effective treatment option."

"Wait a minute." Sidney shook his head. "What cardiologist? Nash hasn't seen a doctor in years, and as far as I know, he isn't on any prescription medication."

Dr Colter suddenly looked very uncomfortable. "I'm sorry, Mr Wilks, but Mr Nash had a medical card in his wallet with your name and number as well as Dr Inchman's information."

Sidney felt like he'd been punched in the stomach. "I didn't know."

The doctor nodded his understanding. "It happens sometimes. Patients don't want to worry their loved ones so they keep their health concerns to themselves."

"What caused the arrhythmia?" Sidney asked.

"Hard to say right now. Dr Inchman is sending over Mr Nash's file. I'll know more after I've given it a thorough read through. The important thing is making sure this doesn't happen again. Whatever course of treatment we determine will be most effective. Mr Nash is in for a major lifestyle change."

"If you did the electro…whatever, when would you do that?"

"Soon. Maybe as early as this evening or tomorrow morning."

"Can I see him?"

"I'll have one of the nurses come and get you once we get him upstairs. He'll be in the ICU for now."

Sidney held out his hand. "Thank you, Dr Colter."

The doctor shook Sidney's hand before excusing himself. The moment the doctor left his side, Bobbi,

Ben and Mike came over and sat close to Sidney. Sidney stared at his friends. What should he tell them, that Nash had been hiding a heart condition from him for who knew how long?

* * * *

Sidney sat at Nash's bedside and stared at his partner. It was just as well Nash was asleep because Sidney had no idea what to say to him. Inside he was a mess of emotions. While he was grateful beyond measure that Nash was possibly going to be okay and getting the help he needed, Sidney seethed over the implications of Nash keeping secrets from him.

Bobbi had tried to calm him down earlier, but it hadn't helped. He'd ended up sending everyone home, promising to call them if there were any changes.

Sidney glanced at the monitors. The nurse had told him he could sit with Nash but not to do or say anything that would upset her patient. She had given Sidney the stink-eye when she'd said it. Evidently his anger was obvious to anyone who cared to notice. Okay, so he wouldn't scream at Nash until he was well enough to defend himself, but no way in hell would he let the lies be swept under a rug.

Nash's hand twitched, drawing Sidney's attention. He stood and stared down at Nash's pale, waxy complexion. "Are you waking up?" he asked, brushing Nash's hair off his forehead.

Nash's eyelids fluttered several times before eventually opening. "Hey."

"Hey, yourself." Despite his anger, Sidney swallowed around the lump in his throat. He had the chance he'd begged God for. There would be plenty of time later to concentrate on his anger. For now, Sidney just wanted to celebrate the fact that Nash had survived. "I heard you made a mess in the egg section of the grocery store."

Nash's eyelids drooped before opening again. It was obvious the man was fighting to stay awake. "I thought I was a goner."

"If it hadn't been for the quick-acting store manager you probably would've been." Sidney lowered the side railing and leaned over to brush a kiss across Nash's cracked lips. "I'm going to make it a point to go shake that manager's hand." He kissed Nash again, holding in the wealth of emotions that threatened. "I love you."

"Love you," Nash whispered. He opened his eyes fully and stared up at Sidney. "I'm sorry."

Sidney's throat seized. He nodded and looked away in an attempt to get himself under control. "Do you want me to call your mom?" he eventually asked.

"Am I gonna die?" Nash asked.

"Not if I can help it."

"Then I'll call her when I'm feeling better."

Sidney didn't know whether Nash didn't want Loretta to worry or if he was afraid she'd fly to Chicago and Sidney would be forced to deal with her. Either way, Sidney approved of Nash's plan. "Okay." Sidney rubbed Nash's cheek with his thumb. "I haven't called Butch. He'll want to come up here, but I'm not ready to be around anyone yet."

"That's okay."

"No it's not. It's selfish. I'll call him here in a little bit."

"You look tired," Nash said.

"Is that another way of saying I look like shit? Because I don't doubt it. You've put me through a wringer today."

"You should let Butch and Luke come and get you."

"I don't plan on going anywhere anytime soon." Sidney kissed Nash again. He pressed his cheek against Nash's. "I don't think the nurse likes me very much. Maybe she doesn't approve of our lifestyle."

"Or maybe she just doesn't like guys with long hair. Don't assume," Nash admonished.

"You're right. See? This is why I need you to take better care of yourself. I'd be a real bastard without you."

"Got that right." Nash's eyelids started to droop again.

"Get some rest. I'll be here when you wake up."

"I don't want to sleep. What if I don't wake up?"

For the first time since he'd been escorted into the room, tears filled Sidney's eyes. "You'd better, because I can't live without you." Sidney had said it before many times but it didn't make it any less true.

* * * *

Butch handed Sidney a small duffle bag. "I put Nash's toothbrush and stuff in there as well."

"Thanks." Sidney set the bag down beside the sofa he'd staked out for himself in the ICU waiting room. "I don't know if they're going to let me stay up here after visiting hours, but I can always go downstairs to the main lobby if I need to."

"And do what? Sleep in a chair?" Luke asked.

"Nash did it for me after the accident."

"And I'd do it for you," Butch told Luke, taking his hand.

Sidney had never got used to the sight of the big bald biker whispering words of love to his best friend. It spoke volumes for Nash's ability to look beyond a person's appearance to get to the goodness they held inside.

"Did you know that Nash's been having trouble with his heart?" he asked Butch.

Butch shook his head. "Your call was the first I'd heard about it."

"He's been under a lot of stress lately. If I find out his job's the reason for all this, he'll never trade another stock," Sidney proclaimed.

"He loves his job." Butch released Luke's hands and leaned towards Sidney, resting his forearms on his knees. "I know this isn't going to be easy for you to hear, but I'm going to say it before you screw shit up with Nash."

"What?" Sidney crossed his arms defensively.

"Nash's already given up one job he loved because of you. Don't push him into a corner with this one."

Sidney felt as though he'd been slapped.

"Butch," Luke said, putting a hand on Butch's shoulder.

"I'm sorry," Butch said over his shoulder. "But he needs to hear this." He turned back to Sidney. "You have a career that you're proud of, well, Nash finally has one, too. Yeah, he may need to make some changes in the way he works, but his job is no less important to him than yours is to you. So unless you're prepared to give up your career you can't ask him to give up his."

"But is a career that could kill him worth it to him?"

"I can't answer that. I'm just trying to make you understand that it has to be his choice, not yours." Butch stood and pulled Sidney to his feet and into the first embrace the big guy had ever given Sidney. "I'm sorry. I know it hurts to realise that you can't protect him from himself, but that's the way it is."

"Kinda like Josh," Luke added. "We all wish he would wake up and stop trying to kill himself with drugs, but we can't do it for him."

Sidney held on as tight as he could, hoping to soak up as much of Butch's strength as possible. "It still doesn't get him off the hook for keeping all this from me."

"I know, and when the time comes I'll kick his ass for you if you want me to," Butch said.

Sidney released Butch and stepped back. "Oh, no, that pleasure will be all mine."

* * * *

Nash watched as Sidney went over the discharge papers with the nurse. He'd done a lot of thinking in the last six days and had settled on a game plan for the future. According to the doctor, the electrical cardioversion seemed to do what they'd hoped, but Nash still had a list of changes he'd need to make concerning his lifestyle. Every time Sidney walked into the hospital room Nash had expected to get an earful about everything he'd tried so hard to hide from him, but thus far, Sidney hadn't said a word about it.

Nash wasn't stupid. He knew a storm was brewing deep inside Sidney. The only question was when it would break free.

"All set," Sidney said, turning back to Nash.

"Great. Get me outta here." Nash had already grudgingly agreed to be taken downstairs in a wheelchair and the damn thing was starting to hurt his ass. "I have no idea how Luke can stand to sit in one of these damn things all day."

"I don't know for sure, but I kinda doubt he has much feeling in his ass." Sidney pushed the elevator button.

"According to Butch, Luke's got plenty of feeling where he needs it." Nash chuckled at Sidney's surprised expression. "What? You didn't think Butch and I talked?"

"About sex? No." The doors opened and Sidney pushed Nash inside. "You don't talk about us, do you?"

"Not much." Nash grinned up at Sidney. "Just an occasional tit for tat."

Although they were alone in the elevator, Sidney bent down and whispered in Nash's ear. "Do not discuss my tits or tats with that man again. Understand?"

The doors slid open just in time to save Nash from answering. Sidney pushed him over to the double doors. "I'll bring the car around."

"I can walk to the car," Nash told him.

"I'll. Bring. The. Car. Around." Sidney pronounced each word in a tone that left Nash slack jawed.

Oh, fuck, the wind was starting to blow. Nash wondered if he'd make it home before the storm hit. "Okay."

"Thank you." Sidney walked out the sliding glass doors and disappeared into the parking lot.

Nash dug his phone out of the plastic sack that contained his personal belongings. He kept one eye on the parking lot as he called Butch.

"Hey, they springing you today?" Butch asked upon answering.

"Yeah. Quick question. How much trouble am I in with Sidney?"

"Duck and cover, buddy," Butch said.

Sidney's shiny black BMW pulled up outside the doors. "Oops, gotta go." Nash ended the call and quickly stuck his cell back in the sack. "All set?"

"Your chariot awaits," Sidney said with a dramatic bow.

Nash smiled. Despite the coming storm, he couldn't help but think the man in front of him was the cutest damn thing he'd ever seen. "Take me home, babe."

Sidney pushed Nash's wheelchair to the sedan. Nash stood up and leaned over to give Sidney a quick kiss. He might as well get as many kisses in as he could.

Sidney smiled before stepping back. "I'll just run this back inside."

Nash climbed into the passenger seat and buckled his seat belt. He owed Sidney an explanation for hiding the truth about his medical condition, but should he jump right in or wait until Sidney was calmer.

Sidney got behind the wheel and slammed the door.

Nash winced. On second thoughts, perhaps calm before the storm was just wishful thinking. However, upsetting Sidney as he drove them both home wasn't an option either. Nash decided to keep his mouth shut until they were safely behind closed doors.

Although it was a relatively short drive, Nash couldn't stop glancing at the clock.

"You late for something?" Sidney asked.

"No. Just looking forward to getting home."

"I'm going the speed limit. Would you like to drive?"

Nash held up his hands. "No. I'm sorry. I didn't mean it like that." Although he understood why

Sidney was angry, Nash was starting to feel a little hot under the collar himself.

He spent the rest of the ride staring out the passenger window. The moment Sidney pulled into the garage and turned off the engine, Nash opened his door. He grabbed the plastic sack from the floorboard and travelled the few steps to the house.

In the kitchen, Nash took a bottle of water from the refrigerator and went straight through to the living room. If he was going to have a long drawn-out argument, he might as well get comfortable.

Sidney came into the living room and gestured to the plastic bag Nash had used for his dirty clothes. "Do you want me to throw those in the washer?"

Nash took a deep breath and shook his head. "What I want is for you to come over here and sit by me."

"I have things to do. I've barely been here for days."

"Please?" Nash asked.

Sidney sat down beside Nash but far enough away that they didn't touch. "Do you need anything?"

"Yeah. I need to talk to you, and I need you to sit still long enough for me to do that."

"I don't think this is the time. You just got out of the hospital."

Nash pulled Sidney against his side and wrapped an arm around him. "I know I hurt you deeply by not being honest with you, and I can't stand the tension I feel between us."

"Why'd you do it?" Sidney asked.

"Because I was afraid if I told you it would make it true. And because I knew I'd done it to myself." It had been Nash's private shame for months before he'd finally collapsed in the supermarket.

"You blindsided me," Sidney mumbled, pulling out of Nash's embrace. "When Dr Colter started talking about you I felt like he was talking about a stranger." Sidney bowed his head. "I would've been there for you, you know? You've always been there for me, and the *one time* I could've been the one with the broad shoulders, you cut me out. It makes me feel like you don't think you can count on me."

"No!" Nash yelled, cutting Sidney off. "I was afraid of what it would do to you if you knew."

"I may be small, but I've been through a lot of shit in my life and managed to come out on the other side. Sure, I wouldn't have been as successful at it without you, but I'm strong. Why don't you believe in me?"

"I do." Nash didn't know how to get through to Sidney. He was screwing up the explanation and didn't know how to get it back on track. "I love you so much that the thought of hurting you was out of the question. I truly believed it would be better to just take the medication and try to manage it myself without worrying you. Was I wrong? Hell yes, but I never expected to keel over in the grocery store."

Sidney nodded. "Are you hiding anything else from me?"

Nash shook his head. "You already know about the diet pills and muscle building supplements. That's it."

Sidney licked his lips. "Okay."

"So you forgive me?" Nash asked.

Sidney was quiet for several moments. "No, at least not yet, but I feel better." He pointed his finger at Nash. "Don't ever fucking shut me out like that again."

"Never," Nash promised. He'd probably be in the dog house for a while longer, but at least everything was finally out in the open.

Chapter Seven

November 1998

Sidney woke at dawn and stretched his arms over his head. He rolled to his side and propped his head up on his hand so he could better watch Nash all warm and dreamy. Neither of them had got much sleep the night before, having stayed up late to greet their guests who had come into town early.

Like he did every morning when he woke, Sidney leaned over and kissed Nash's chest, just above his heart, silently thanking the stupid organ for giving Nash another day. *Time to get up,* he told himself.

He carefully tossed back the covers and crawled out of bed before shuffling into the bathroom. As he lifted the toilet seat and started a healthy stream, he tried to dig the sleep out of his eyes.

Although he'd made other arrangements for the big brunch, he still had Thanksgiving dinner to prepare. Fortunately he'd used the time the previous evening to bake pies and Luke had promised to come early to peel the potatoes.

Sidney smiled as he pulled on a pair of sweatpants and a T-shirt before heading out of the room. Despite Luke's grumbling the previous year, he didn't like JJ taking his job. He told Sidney it was because he didn't want to be forced into doing the dishes again, but Sidney knew the truth.

He paused beside the guestroom door for a moment before continuing down the stairs. It felt strange to have Josh in the house. Nash hadn't been pleased when Sidney had told him he wanted to invite his old friend. Nash actually called Peter and talked to him about Josh's condition before agreeing to the extended invitation.

Sidney had taken Nash's worry in stride. Nash was simply trying to protect him. It was something he both loved and hated about Nash, but love won out every time. He didn't bother turning on a light as he passed through the living room on his way to the kitchen. There was something about the darkened house that brought him peace. It would be the only time in the next forty-eight hours that he had to himself, and he planned to enjoy it.

He heard a yelp the moment he entered the kitchen. Sidney stopped long enough to turn the coffee pot on before opening the laundry room door. "Morning, Dottie."

The three-month-old YorkiePoo stared up at him and barked. Sidney chuckled and bent over to unlatch the crate. "You need to go potty?"

Sidney grabbed the leash off the wall hook and fastened it to the small gem-studded collar. He took Nash's big coat from another hook and shrugged into it while stepping into his partner's old cowboy boots.

As he walked outside with Dottie, Sidney couldn't help but to feel like a little boy who was dressing in his dad's clothes. He just hoped the neighbours were still asleep. "Go on," he told the puppy.

Nash had surprised Sidney with Dottie a month earlier. He'd told Sidney it was time they settled down and got a dog. Sidney had a feeling it was more than that since he doubted they could get any more settled than they already were.

Nash had let it slip several times that Dottie would make a good companion for Sidney, never bringing his own name into it. Since the heart attack four months earlier, Nash often had quiet spells when he seemed to retreat into his own thoughts for short periods. It was after one of those times that Nash came home with Dottie.

Although he didn't say it, Nash seemed to worry about having another heart attack and leaving Sidney alone. There wasn't a day that went by that Sidney didn't worry about the same thing, but he never mentioned it to Nash.

Sidney glanced down just in time to see Dottie pee on the frozen sidewalk. "Really?" he asked the dog. "I swept that whole area of snow there for you just yesterday."

He'd already determined that such a small dog was going to be a pain in the ass in the winter. Dottie's first reaction to the early snow that had fallen the previous morning was disdain. She'd scrunched up her nose and made herself comfortable on the top of Sidney's feet, refusing to go anywhere near the cold white powder. Sidney had finally taken a broom and swept an area of the grass until Dottie was able to pee without getting her tummy in the snow. "Spoiled brat," he mumbled with affection.

Business done, Dottie started to climb on top of Nash's boots again, but Sidney bent over and scooped her into his arms. He kissed the sweet little head several times on the way back into the house. "You're such a pretty girl."

He was surprised to find Josh in the kitchen pouring a cup of coffee. Josh had arrived late the previous night and they hadn't had a chance to really talk. "Morning," Sidney greeted.

"Morning." Josh blew on his coffee and gestured to Dottie whom he hadn't met. "Is that a dog or a chew toy?"

Sidney held up his pride and joy with one hand. "This is my baby, Dottie. Nash gave her to me as an early birthday present."

"Didn't know you liked dogs." Josh leant back against the island and stared down at the dog when Sidney put her on the floor.

"I've never had one before. Well, I take that back. My dad had a German Shepherd for a little while, but Sheba made the mistake of going after one of the calves, so Dad shot her."

"Damn, that's harsh."

Sidney shrugged. "He said once a dog gets a taste for blood you can't stop them from doing it again."

Josh shifted his weight. "Heard about your dad. I'm not sure whether to give you condolences or congratulations."

Sidney was taken back. He was sure a number of people had felt the same way, but Josh had been the only one to verbalise it. "A little of both, I think." He poured a cup of coffee and pulled the chocolate mint creamer out of the refrigerator. "Want some?"

"No thanks." Josh took a seat on one of the bar stools. "I wanted to talk to you before everyone else got up."

"Okay." Sidney joined Josh at the island and opened the box of pastries he'd purchased the day before. After selecting a cream cheese Danish, he slid the box towards Josh. "First let me say how glad I am to have you here. You've done really well this time."

Josh closed the box without taking one. "Thanks. I've been clean for fourteen months and eleven days." He shook his head. "And still there isn't a day that goes by that I don't want to use."

Besides Nash, the closest thing Sidney had ever been addicted to was cigarettes, and he hadn't really been all that dependent on them. "I don't know what you're going through, but I hope you continue to win that daily battle."

"Me too." Josh stood and refilled his cup. "You know it hurts when you guys shut me out."

"I know it does," Sidney confessed. "But it hurts too much to be around you when you're high."

"I may slip up again," Josh warned.

"I know. That's why it was so important to me to have you here with us this year." Sidney reached over and threaded his fingers through Josh's. "I love you, you stupid idiot. I miss you when you're not yourself."

"This a private party?" Eric asked, coming into the kitchen bare chested. He wrapped his arm around Josh's neck and rubbed the top of Josh's head with his knuckles.

"Get away from me. You stink of sex," Josh said, pushing Eric back.

Eric laughed. "Don't be jealous." He kissed Josh on the cheek and reached for the box of pastries. "Tommy found JJ a job right outside Austin," Eric announced.

"So does that mean you're making the move?" Sidney asked. Eric and JJ had been seeing each other as much as they could since the previous year. When JJ told Tommy he planned to ask Eric to come and live with him on the ranch, Tommy had dissuaded JJ by telling him life would be hard for the two of them in such a small town. Tommy had set about trying to find JJ another ranch closer to a big city.

"Yep," Eric said with a dopey lovesick smile. "If I can't get a transfer, I'll quit and find something else in Austin."

"I'm still not used to seeing you with a dude," Josh grumbled.

"Get over it, bro."

JJ walked into the room and wrapped his arms around Eric. "Morning," he said to the rest of the room.

It seemed Sidney's moment of solitude was over for the day.

* * * *

At eight, Sidney carried a cup of decaffeinated coffee into the bedroom and set it on the table. He took off his clothes and squirted lube onto his fingers. Bending over, Sidney quickly stretched his ass while Nash still lay sleeping.

It wasn't that he didn't love Nash taking the time to tease and play with his hole, but he still had a million things to do before guests started to arrive. After preparing himself, he slid under the covers and pressed his body against Nash, trying to soak up as much of the man's warmth as he could.

"Mmmm," Nash moaned and pulled Sidney closer. "You're cold."

"I've been up for the last three hours, sleepy head."

Nash finally opened his eyes and stared at Sidney. His hand drifted to Sidney's bare ass. "So what're you doing back in bed?"

"Trying to steal a few minutes with the man I love before the craziness begins." Sidney kissed the underside of Nash's stubbled chin.

"I like the sound of that." Nash lifted Sidney's leg to drape over his hip, opening Sidney's ass cheeks enough to touch him.

Nash's fingers travelled immediately to Sidney's lubed hole. "Someone's awfully presumptuous this morning," Nash commented, pushing a finger inside.

"I can leave if you want me to?" Sidney teased. He moved his hips back and forth, fucking himself on Nash's finger.

"Not on your life." Nash tilted Sidney's chin up for a kiss. It was lazy at first, Nash's lips still puffy with sleep, but soon the passion that had always been between them ignited and the kiss became carnal.

Nash bathed Sidney's lips and face with his tongue as he rolled them over, sliding on top. Sidney's hands travelled from Nash's still-thick hair down his back to his butt. He squeezed the muscled cheeks and groaned.

Although Nash had been forced to give up his extreme exercise programme, he'd been able to find alternatives. He now jogged on the treadmill for twenty minutes each morning before moving on to a twenty minute training exercise using resistance bands instead of actual weights. The routine activity had been enough to keep Nash's body in the shape he'd fought so hard to achieve.

Nash reached to the bedside table and grabbed the lube. After slicking his cock, he placed the tip at Sidney's hole. "Ready?"

"I was ready when I got into bed," Sidney reminded him.

"I haven't forgotten. I just didn't know if you were looking for more foreplay before I shoved my dick inside you."

"Not unless you want to put me way behind schedule."

Nash eased his way inside. "You're so romantic."

"My thoughts are romantic. It's just my body that resembles a whore." Sidney sucked in a breath as Nash thrust in to the hilt.

Nash moaned and ground against Sidney. "I like 'em both. Right now I'm really fond of the whore."

Wrapping his legs around Nash's waist, Sidney pulled him down for a kiss. He thoroughly explored the interior of Nash's mouth. After years together, they'd long ago overcome the morning breath issue.

Nash withdrew before thrusting back inside, sending Sidney's body into euphoria. "Fuck me," Sidney begged. He dug his short nails into Nash's back as Nash's big cock pistoned in and out of him at a blurring speed. It felt so good that Sidney was having trouble catching a breath.

Nash slowed his rhythm. "You okay? This old man too much for you this morning?"

Sidney narrowed his eyes. "So good," Sidney panted. "More."

With a deep groan, Nash worked Sidney's ass twice as fast. He continued to stare down at Sidney with a cross between a smile and a grimace on his face.

Sidney hoped the odd expression was out of pleasure and not pain, but he'd learned after Nash was released from the hospital not to question his partner during sex.

The first time he had verbalised his worry that Nash was overexerting himself, Nash had withdrawn and stormed out of the room. Later Sidney had received an earful from Nash on how he didn't want to spend the rest of his life afraid to fuck the way he wanted. He'd told Sidney in no uncertain terms that if he had another attack, he only prayed it was while driving deep and hard inside Sidney and not in the damn refrigerated section of the grocery store. Since then, Sidney had accepted everything Nash gave him with a smile.

Sidney's mouth opened wide as he cried out his release. Nash surprised him by tickling the roof of Sidney's mouth with his tongue. The two sensations worked off each other to make his climax more powerful. His body jerked with the intensity of his pleasure.

Nash continued his arduous rhythm for several moments before succumbing to his own fulfilment. With a contented sigh, he collapsed on top of Sidney with his cock still buried deep.

Sidney played with Nash's sweaty hair as his partner's laboured breathing slowly returned to normal.

"Wow," Nash said.

"Yeah," Sidney agreed.

* * * *

Once again, Nash and Butch were on table duty. There would be a slightly smaller group for Thanksgiving dinner, so the set-up was a breeze.

Peter and Bobbi were due to be picked up from the airport just before dinner, after a short trip to visit Bobbi's parents in New York.

"So what's up with having the brunch tomorrow at the Crystal Palace?" Butch asked, handing one side of the plastic tablecloth to Nash.

"Sidney decided to spring for a caterer instead of making brunch himself." Nash shrugged. "Truthfully, I think he's just trying to go easy on me this year."

"Good for him." Butch settled the tablecloth and tried to smooth out a few wrinkles. "It's not like the two of you don't have the money, so why bust your asses when you don't have to."

Nash had made up everything he'd lost a year ago and had almost doubled their savings in the process. *God bless the dot coms.* After he'd returned from the hospital, he'd had a long talk with Peter about the stress involved in the volatile market. Peter had suggested Nash just sit back and give his investments time to stabilise and to only stick with the companies he truly believed in. The outcome had been incredible. Nash currently worked three or four hours a day, spending the rest of his time reading newspapers and magazines. At first he thought he was being lazy, but he'd learned more about the current and supposed future trends than he ever would've watching the stock boards.

"We have enough," Nash finally said in answer to Butch's statement. Truth be told, he'd begun to stockpile money in case of his untimely death—not that he didn't believe Sidney would continue to thrive in his career, but it was a source of comfort for Nash to know his beloved would never again have financial worries.

"By the way, thanks a lot for putting the idea of getting a dog into Luke's head. He's talked about nothing else lately." Butch handed Nash another deep yellow tablecloth.

"Actually, although I bought Dottie for Sidney, I've enjoyed her company during the day. With Luke working from home most days, it might not be a bad idea."

"Do you really see me loving on a rat-sized dog?"

Nash tried to imagine a man of Butch's size holding Dottie. "No. Can't say that I do, but nothing says the dog has to be small. As protective as you are, I'm surprised you haven't bought Luke a big guard dog."

Butch's eyes lit up. "Like a Shepherd or Doberman. Damn, why didn't I think of that? I'd be able to work late without worrying about Luke being home alone after dark."

Nash chuckled. Butch often took his protective tendencies to the extreme, something Nash knew had caused a few problems between the two men in the past. "Just do yourself a favour and don't tell Luke why you're buying such a big dog."

"I'm not dumb. I'll tell him I need a bigger dog that can handle some rough play. He'll understand," Butch said with a wink.

Nash held his hands out. "No more. Sidney told me I wasn't allowed to swap sex stories with you anymore."

"Well I guess I'll have to find another best friend." Butch settled the last tablecloth into place before turning towards the door. "I bet JJ will swap stories with me. I wonder how alike the two brothers are?"

"Shut the fuck up." Nash threw a wad of trash at Butch, hitting his friend in the back before he'd made it out the door.

* * * *

Shortly after dinner, Nash walked into the kitchen and over to Sidney who was sitting at the kitchen table enjoying the Ballentine brothers' spectacle. "Hey, babe."

Sidney tilted his head back for a kiss, noticing the dark circles under Nash's eyes. He smoothed a hand down Nash's handsome face and smiled. "You feeling okay?"

"Tired. I think I'm going to sneak upstairs and lie down for a while."

"You want me to come?" Sidney asked.

Nash grinned. "I'm not likely to get much rest if I get you alone now am I?"

Sidney nipped Nash's bottom lip. "Probably not. Go on, I'll wake you before we start on round two." Leftovers had always been Nash's favourite part of Thanksgiving dinner.

"Food was good."

"Thanks." Sidney gave Nash another quick kiss before reaching around to swat him on the butt. "Go take a nap."

After Nash left the room, Maggie walked over and sat beside Sidney. "I'm proud of you."

"What?" Sidney asked.

"You don't hover over him although I know you'd like to," she said.

Sidney shrugged. "It would hurt his pride."

"I know, but I wonder if he understands how much strength it takes to watch someone you love struggle and not try to help every minute of the day."

"You speak from personal experience," he recognised.

"I do," she acknowledged. "Although I'm not nearly as strong as you are." Tears filled Maggie's eyes as she turned to watch her sons argue. "I've driven one son away already, and I'm afraid of doing the same to Josh."

"They're two different people, Maggie. I think Josh needs the attention. He probably always has. He'll let you know when you need to lighten up."

"I hope you're right. It almost killed me when Luke moved here." She sighed and dabbed the corners of her eyes with a napkin. "But I see now he made the right move. Butch is…"

"Scary looking?" Sidney offered.

"Yes. But he's also the best thing that's ever happened to Luke. I don't think I could've picked a better partner for my son."

"He dotes on him," Sidney added.

Maggie nodded, as another stray tear trickled down her ageing cheek.

"Are you making my mom cry?" Eric asked, walking over to punch Sidney in the arm.

Sidney reached up and gave Eric's nipple a hard twist. "No, I'm not. Leave your fists to yourself."

"They're happy tears," Maggie interjected.

Eric looked at Maggie and shook his head. "Women are so weird. No wonder it took a man to finally make me feel good enough to commit."

Maggie covered her ears and rolled her eyes. "I'm not listening to this," she trilled in a sing-song voice.

Eric laughed. "She's just mad because she figured I'd be the one to provide her with a grandchild."

"And instead it's going to be me. I'll be the new favourite and the rest of you can go to the back of the line," Peter announced from across the kitchen.

Sidney's jaw dropped. He narrowed his eyes at Peter. "Where's Bobbi?"

"Watching football with the men while I do the dishes."

Maggie jumped from her chair and rushed over to hug Peter. "I'm so happy for you, darling. I need to go congratulate Bobbi."

Sidney put a hand on Maggie's shoulder. "I need to have a talk with her first."

"Don't you go in there and try to warn her away from me," Peter said with a scowl.

"Do you remember the promise you gave me last year?" Sidney asked.

"I remember."

"Good." Sidney left the kitchen and walked straight to Bobbi. Grabbing her hand, he hauled her to her feet. "We need to talk."

"Uh oh," Bobbi said, as Sidney dragged her towards the front door.

Sidney hadn't realised until they were outside that he'd forgotten coats. "Garage," he ordered.

Bobbi saluted. "Yes, sir."

The moment they were in the heated garage with the door shut, Sidney wrapped his arms around one of his best friends. "Why didn't you tell me? Is that the reason you went to New York?"

"I was planning to, and yes." Bobbi's face was positively glowing with happiness. "I found out towards the end of September, but I didn't want to jinx anything by telling anyone too soon. Well, except for Peter, of course."

Sidney laughed. "So that Labor Day vacation took on a totally new meaning for the two of you."

"Yes!" Bobbi pumped her arms into the air. She lowered them and gazed at Sidney. "I'm so happy."

"I assume you'll be getting married, right?"

Bobbi rolled her eyes. "God, Sidney, not even my dad asked us that."

"That doesn't surprise me. You're dad's a damn hippy. Now answer the question."

"Yes, we're planning to have something simple on New Year's Eve."

"And what about moving? Peter promised me he wouldn't take you away from me." Sidney would be upset if Bobbi followed Peter to Philadelphia but he'd get over it as long as they came to Chicago for Thanksgiving.

"He's already put his townhouse up for sale." Bobbi suddenly giggled and clapped her hands, bouncing up and down on the balls of her feet. "I'm getting married!"

Sidney wrapped his arms around her again and hugged her. "I'm so happy for you." As he rested his chin on Bobbi's shoulder, Sidney looked around the room. As much work as it was to have Thanksgiving at his house every year, it seemed to be a magical location for bringing the people he cared most about closer together.

"I bet Ben will make you stop going on job sites while you're pregnant," Sidney said, pulling away.

"I bet he *won't*," Bobbi stated emphatically.

"We'll see." Sidney wasn't the only one at Creative Solutions who had a soft spot for the redhead. He figured Bobbi was in for seven months of overprotective co-workers.

* * * *

Sidney made a point after most of the leftovers had been consumed to get a few quiet moments with JJ. "How's the ranch doing?"

"Good. You don't have to worry about Tommy. He knows what he's doing," JJ said.

"I've never worried about Tommy. He loves that ranch as much as Nash does."

"And you? Do you love it?"

Sidney took a deep breath and studied his younger brother. It still amazed him that they looked nothing like each other even though they shared the same father. Although it had bothered him at first, it hadn't taken more than a couple of conversations with JJ to see the good heart behind the blond hair and tall frame.

Sidney measured his words carefully. "I love the idea of the ranch. I take comfort knowing my mom and Grandpa and Grandma Running Elk are buried there, but there isn't a single thing about ranch life that I like aside from swimming in the creek. Don't get me wrong, the Running E will always hold a special place in my heart, but I don't think of it as my home, I never have. Nash is my home."

"How come you always manage to say the right thing? I've been pretty nervous lately about leaving Kansas to take the job in Texas, but you just made me feel so much better."

It was nice to see JJ in love mode. "Are you trying to tell me that Eric is your home?"

"Yeah. It scares me though because what if I'm just a novelty? It'd just be my luck to give up my job and move to Texas and then find out Eric's worked the gay out of his system and is back to women."

Sidney scooted over and rested his head against JJ's shoulder. "That's your insecurities talking. Believe me, I know all about them."

"He's so hot. He could have anyone he wants."

"You're right. And yet you're the first man he's ever been attracted to and the first person he's ever fallen in love with." Sidney ruffled JJ's blond hair. "And not to bring you down, little brother, but Eric's slept with a *lot* of women. Yet here he is, in my house with you, willing to give up everything he has to share a life with you. I think you owe it to yourself and to him to give each other that chance."

JJ leaned over and kissed the top of Sidney's head. "I wish I'd known you when I was younger."

"Yeah. Me too." Sidney decided he quite enjoyed this big brother thing.

* * * *

Nash studied the room. Two walls of glass allowed the picturesque landscape outside to become a part of the interior decoration. The tables were covered in linen tablecloths and the crystal and china of the dishes. It was all extraordinarily beautiful but cold at the same time.

Despite his years of bitching, Nash enjoyed the large gathering in the garage at their house. Finding enough room for all Sidney's invited guests became almost a puzzle to be figured out each year. Nash had no idea he'd miss the yearly brunch game until he'd arrived at the Crystal Palace.

While Sidney fussed with the floral arrangements artfully displayed on each table, Nash sat at a table in the back corner of the room and sipped his decaffeinated coffee. Sidney glanced up from his most recent task and met Nash's gaze.

Nash tried to give his partner the best smile he could muster, hoping it would be enough. Sidney's sudden look of concern told him without words he hadn't been successful.

Sidney walked over to the table and rested a hand on Nash's shoulder. "Something wrong?"

"No." Nash lifted Sidney's hand and kissed it. Sidney had worked too hard on the celebration for Nash to put any kind of dampener on the occasion.

Sidney insinuated himself between Nash and the table and sat in his lap. With his hands clasped behind Nash's neck, Sidney continued to stare at Nash. "Talk to me, and don't bother trying to tell me nothing's wrong because I can tell there is."

"I feel fine if that's what you're worried about." Nash ran his hand up and down Sidney's back. "Honest."

Sidney shook his head. "Tell me."

Nash sighed. "This place is incredibly beautiful, but it doesn't make me feel the same as I do at home."

Sidney dropped one arm and turned to survey the room. "You think I should've ordered darker tablecloths?"

"No. It's not the room or the decorations."

"Then what is it?"

Nash wished he could put his finger on it. Since he'd brought it up, he felt Sidney deserved an answer. "I don't know. I guess maybe it's because we don't have any memories here. It just doesn't feel like a home."

"Like a garage you mean?"

Nash chuckled. "Yeah, but..." Nash sighed. "It seems kinda fancy. Can you imagine Alan unbuttoning his top button after he leaves the table here like he does at home?"

Sidney caught a case of the giggles. "I remember the first Thanksgiving I spent at their house. Only back then, Alan unbuttoned before he even left the dinner table. It's always infuriated Maggie, but Alan calms her down by telling her to stop cooking such good food and he wouldn't be forced to eat so much."

Nash gestured to the opulent surroundings. "How comfortable do you think he'll be here? Don't you think he'd rather be cramped at our house?"

"It's a little late to be voicing your opinion on this, Nash. You're the one who told me last year that I wasn't allowed to invite any more people without finding a different location."

"I know, and I was wrong. Maybe instead of finding an alternate location next year, you should design an addition to the house that we could add this spring."

"Really?" Sidney asked, wiggling his ass against Nash's hardening cock.

"It makes the most sense. We've got plenty of yard space for an addition on the back, and I imagine we could get a pretty good rate on the construction. Unless of course, the Shriver brothers don't want to get invited to brunch in the future."

The doors opened and Luke and Butch entered. Nash gave Sidney's ass a playful squeeze. "Go greet your guests."

"Are you sure you'll be okay suffering through brunch here?"

Feeling overly sentimental, Nash pulled Sidney's head down for a deep kiss. "Never, in all the years I've known you have I suffered with you at my side."

* * * *

Sidney cracked the burnt sugary top of his crème brûlée and sank his spoon into the creamy centre. He moaned as the first bite coated his tongue. "Damn, this is good."

Beside him, Nash shrugged. "It's okay, but I liked those little lemon tart things you made last year better."

Sidney grinned. Although Nash hadn't made a big deal out of it, each time Sidney complimented the food, Nash would find something that Sidney made better. It might annoy some people, but Sidney took it in his stride. Overall, the food had been absolutely fantastic, far surpassing anything Sidney had ever served.

"I know you're trying to be nice, but I've never made crème brûlée like this in my life," Sidney said, taking another bite.

"Look around, babe. Do you think anyone here really cares that you can't make crème brûlée? They've never come to brunch for the food anyway."

Sidney watched his friends and family as he finished his dessert. It felt strange to be seated so far away from the people he loved. He'd enjoyed sitting with JJ, Eric, Butch and Luke, but he wasn't close enough to hear Zac talk about law school or Maggie reprimand Alan for putting his elbows on the table.

Looking around, he knew he wasn't the only one who felt it. The room was too quiet. In a split-second decision, Sidney stood up and tapped his spoon against his champagne flute. "May I have your attention please," he said, loud enough for everyone to hear.

All eyes turned towards him.

"I'd like to thank you all for coming, but I have a very important request." He held up his finger. "However, before I announce my request, I'd like to take this opportunity to tell you all how much you mean to me. It's been a hard year for us, but thankfully we had all of you to help me and Nash through it. And I want each and every one of you to know that I may not say it enough, but you truly are my family, and I love each and every one of you." Sidney chuckled. "Well, except Mike's date who I haven't really got a chance to know yet, but I'm sure by this time next year I'll not only know your name but I may even ask you to peel potatoes."

The room erupted in laughter.

"I would like to ask you all to please stand up."

It took several moments, but eventually every stood. "Now, if you would kindly move your chairs out of the way, I would like to see how many tables we can cluster together to make one giant table for all of us to sit at."

Laughter and conversation filled the room as everyone came together to rearrange the formal seating layout into one which created a more casual atmosphere. Squished together, elbow to elbow, Sidney blew a kiss to everyone. "That's much better. Thank you."

Seated once again, Sidney leaned over and kissed Nash on the cheek. "You were right. It's not as much fun without dodging Butch's elbow as he eats."

"I have a feeling you just made everyone a lot happier," Nash said, giving Sidney a soft kiss.

Sidney was soon caught up in a conversation with Mike and his new boyfriend...Shane. He felt Nash squeeze his thigh and glanced over to find his partner's expression completely transformed. Nash looked truly happy for the first time since they'd arrived at the Crystal Palace. Sidney had learned his lesson. Never again would he assume bigger and more expensive meant better.

His friends and family loved him regardless. Whether they were crowded together in a garage for Thanksgiving dinner or sitting with him at the hospital while he yelled one moment and cried the next, he knew he could always count on them. And for that, he'd gladly stand in the kitchen for two days every November.

About the Author

An avid reader for years, one day Carol Lynne decided to write her own brand of erotic romance. Carol juggles between being a full-time mother and a full-time writer. These days, you can usually find Carol either cleaning jelly out of the carpet or nestled in her favourite chair writing steamy love scenes.

Carol Lynne loves to hear from readers.

You can find her contact information, website details and author profile page at http://www.total-e-bound.com.

Total-E-Bound Publishing

www.total-e-bound.com

Take a look at our exciting range of literagasmic™
erotic romance titles and discover pure quality
at Total-E-Bound.

CPSIA information can be obtained at www.ICGtesting.com
Printed in the USA
BVOW060259010312

284181BV00001B/21/P